To Siti and [

you enjoy the book as much I hope

as we enjoy you!

Regards, Nigel

May.
2019

MALACCA MYSTERY

NIGEL SMITH

ISBN-13: 978-1-945532-80-1

Library of Congress Control Number: 2018958703

Publishing, Editing, and Cover Design by:
Opportune Independent Publishing Co.
113 N. Live Oak Street
Houston, TX 77003
(832) 263-1700
www.opportunepublishing.com

For more information about the author please visit and contact:

www.pinkstafford.com
info@pinkstafford.com

CONTENTS

CHAPTER 1

The warm tropical water was cloudy with fine sediment; visibility was virtually nil. Below the calm surface, an oilfield diver was trying to grope his way along a pipeline, hand over hand. His dive light, a futile glow in the murk, was useless in such conditions. Two of the divers had followed the anchor chain of a marker buoy down to where the latest well in the Padang oil field met the seabed some twenty meters beneath the surface. From this place, the precious bounty of crude oil was piped to a central gathering facility on the nearby mainland. They roped together. One stayed behind and payed out line to the other, who cautiously followed the pipe away from the wellhead.

Both divers were apprehensive from horror stories of this terrible area. They knew seven lives had been lost in these waters, probably more. Their Indonesian colleagues related horrific tales of Jin, the spirit-world monster who lurked in this channel. Getting the crew to work on the rigs and oil-production facilities here was always a difficult task. Problems had occurred since the project's inception five years ago. Crew members began dying, most of them in this silty water.

The worst thing for the divers was the poor visibility. It was difficult to see their hands even just a couple of centimeters in front of their masks.

Dan, the lead diver, cursed again and wondered about his decision to go ahead despite the sinister reputation of the area.

He also muttered obscenities at the current. Although they were diving at slack tide, the movement of water around the nearby island and through the channel meant that there was always some residual current, and both divers expended effort holding themselves against it. Grimly, Dan struggled on astride the pipe that he could not see until his hands felt a fingerlike protrusion from a collar surrounding the pipe.

This surprised him, as the plans he had studied before the dive showed clear pipe for another twenty meters or so. With his free hand, he examined the protrusion. It was about ten centimeters long, as round as his thumb, and made of metal at the base with a flexible rubber top. He grabbed it for balance and began feeling further around the pipe; he found another and then another.

Then something snatched his free arm near the shoulder. Searing pain exploded in his body as something else struck his face, ripping his mask off and biting into his skin. His body contorted in agony, and his mind blacked out as water rushed into his lungs.

Mick, his partner, tensed as the line he had been feeding out slowly for the last fifteen minutes jerked suddenly and then went slack. Now it was pulling gently, but something was wrong. There was no life at the end; it felt like inert mass being carried by the current.

Quickly, Mick gathered the line in, his mind racing. He instinctively knew something terrible had happened to his friend. Dan was too experienced to panic or do anything foolish. Something must have taken him, and there was Mick, pulling its prey and whatever *it* was closer to himself.

At that thought, he froze. He then quickly clipped the end of the spool to the wellhead and shot to the surface as fast as his training and experience would allow.

The midday equatorial sun beat down savagely on the *Bintang Laut*; all aboard were sweating profusely. She was a traditional Indonesian *pinisi*, or sailing yawl, converted to her new role as a diving vessel. Despite her ancient lines, she had two powerful and well-maintained diesels below and could do a respectable rate of knots if required. Her fifteen-meter length was well-utilized, containing a decompression chamber, bottle racks, air compressor, and all the paraphernalia of a diving vessel. Attention was focused near the bow, where a space had been cleared, and a black goat was bound in the center of a circle of dark Indonesian men, five of them in diving gear. A drum was beating slowly, a droll macabre beat.

The leader of the divers gazed intently into the water. He had a red sash around his neck outside of his thick neoprene wetsuit; the others were adorned similarly. He turned his leathery, sun-blackened face to the captain and signaled his readiness; it was the time of slack water. The drum began to beat louder and quicker, and the captain lifted a long, deadly machete toward the sun. He was a burly, stumpy man with a dark, scarred face and expressionless black eyes. He grasped the handle with both hands, feet apart, the blade glinting. Two other men brought the goat to him. Its mouth was frothing white with fright, but it was helpless in its bindings. One man held its hindquarters while the other grabbed its head, and together they straightened out its neck.

The drum was now beating feverishly, but the captain stood rock solid, implacable. Then, when he detected the right striking line, the machete slid through the air and down. The head of the goat parted from the body cleanly, but before much crimson blood had seeped onto the deck, the carcass was lifted up and taken to the side. The muddy brown water below became tinted red as the animal's life drained into it. Each diver then entered the water through the scarlet cloud as more blood rained down upon them. When all five had checked their equipment and made last-minute adjustments, the leader gave a sign and led the way out of the crimson area to the marker buoy near the dive boat. One by one, they disappeared down the mooring chain as the lifeless goat was tied securely to the vessel's side, only to be removed when they returned. Their mission was to retrieve another victim of Jin.

Terry glimpsed Dan's body as it passed through the small production platform to the helipad. As the body could not be retrieved until some twenty-four hours after Mick had burst to the surface, the swirling currents had tangled his corpse in the loose line. During that time, the flesh had softened, and the thin safety line had torn through the wetsuit and the body, causing the face to become a grisly mess.

Terry shuddered at its grossly contorted appearance. The medical crew wrapped it in cloth and plastic and placed it in the waiting helicopter.

The doors were closed, and the pilot turned over the first engine. A slow whine soon became a high-pitched roar and clatter as the turbine began turning and built up rapidly to normal speed. The second engine was then started and checked before the all-clear was given, and the ungainly craft lifted and swooped off, taking its cacophony with it.

He watched the chopper disappear over the treetops and then walked down to the mess, hands thrust deeply into the pockets of his overalls and head bowed in thought.

CHAPTER 2

⚓

Terry Miles was a reservoir engineer and worked for Exacom Oil. His expertise was assessing how much oil could be produced from a particular field and then optimizing production in the most cost-effective way. Although he worked for an American oil company, he was born and raised in Brewster, a small town in the Gippsland of Victoria, Australia. Due to its close location to Bass Strait, many of the companies involved with servicing the oil platforms of the strait had established their operations bases in Brewster. Terry had grown up surrounded by the workings of the oil industry and the circulation of foreign workers through the town.

Like many young Australians, he had the privilege of a childhood spent in a stable, secure environment. His parents were also from the Gippsland and owned the Miles Newsagent in Brewster. Consequently, there was no shortage of reading material in the Miles household. Life revolved around the business, and his parents always seemed occupied with it as they struggled to raise Terry and his two sisters. Despite the demands on their time, both parents appreciated the value of spending time with their children. They read to them from an early age, they encouraged them in various sports, and the family enjoyed many excursions to the abundant natural attractions in Brewster's hinterland. A strong bond had developed among the family members.

Terry also spent his testosterone-pumped teenage years

in Brewster, at the local high school, where the innocence of an idyllic childhood vanished, to be replaced by pimples, drinking, girls, insecurity, and peer pressure to do stupid things. Like most, he somehow survived the teenage state despite the exasperation of his parents. He also seemed to do enough work to get through school and showed strength in math and science.

High school finally finished, and the after-exam parties started. Terry conceived a stunt during one after-exam party that ensured him and his friends a place in Brewster folklore. One of his friends, Mat, had left school when he was fifteen to take up a motor mechanic apprenticeship at Mason's Automotive, one of only two automotive shops in town. He had grown up on a nearby farm and had been playing with engines most of his life. Mat had come along to the gathering of his former schoolmates and boasted that he could "strip the donger out of a Commodore in forty-five minutes." An idea seeded itself in Terry's head, which he described to his mates. All seven swore an oath of secrecy and made their plans.

One hot summer night, during a particularly warm week before Christmas, Sergeant Spanders returned to his weatherboard house after the normal nightly cruise around the town. As his family was asleep, he grabbed a beer from the fridge, turned on the television, slumped into an easy chair, and quickly went to sleep himself. He didn't notice the roof of his cruiser slip by the kitchen window on its way out of the driveway.

Next morning after breakfast, he waved goodbye to his wife, slipped into his car, turned the ignition, and nothing happened. He tried again, and nothing happened in exactly the same way it had not happened the first time.

"Shit," he swore as he released the hood catch and hauled himself outside.

"What's the problem?" called his wife from the kitchen

window.

"Bloody car won't start."

He raised the hood, then his jaw dropped, and his eyes bulged. His right hand went limp, and the hood slammed back shut on his other hand, causing him to cry out in pain.

"Are you all right?" called his wife.

"I dunno. I think someone's stolen my engine."

"What do you mean? Don't be ridiculous."

"Come out here and see for yourself."

Out she came in her pink flannel dressing gown and fluffy slippers. He slowly opened the hood again, and they peered inside, eyes wide.

"Who the bloody hell…"

Just then the police radio burst to life.

"Mobile one, mobile one, Sergeant Spanders, will you come in, please?" the sergeant started, and for the second time, the hood slammed back shut. Bewildered, the policeman grabbed the handpiece from inside the car and called in.

"Brewster base, this is Sergeant Spanders."

"Sergeant Spanders, I thought that I should tell you, sir, that when I opened the office this morning, I found an engine on a pallet in the reception area. It has a blue ribbon tied around it."

Sergeant Spanders was furious and raged around the town trying to find the culprits but without success. The problem was that nobody else in the town could keep a straight face about the incident, which made a serious investigation very difficult. There were no fingerprints on the car or engine, and no witnesses willing to come forward.

Mason offered to put the police car back together again and also offered Sergeant Spanders twelve months of free service on his own car. (Unknown to the sergeant, one apprentice performed this work unpaid.) A "sorry" card, a bottle of Johnnie Walker, and a bouquet of flowers also appeared on the roof of his police car the next week. Sergeant Spanders was mollified, and the town moved on again. Brewster had a habit of solving its problems in its own way.

Terry had moved from Brewster early in 1977 to Melbourne, where he studied engineering at Monash University. He specialized in petroleum engineering and was recruited by Exacom in Melbourne, where he worked for three years. Moving away from his hometown seemed to trigger a curiosity and thirst for the rest of the world. The expatriate Americans often talked of their other overseas assignments, and Terry listened with growing interest. As he matured, the small pond of life in Brewster became less of a focus in his consciousness, and his interest shifted to the rest of the world. He realized that there was a lot of other life out there, and he grew more to want a part of it.

When Exacom advertised internally for petroleum engineers to go to Indonesia, where they had been having a good deal of explorative success, Terry jumped at the opportunity. He filled out applications, went to interviews, and participated in a teleconference link with Houston. To his delight, he was offered a position in Jakarta, where he joined many other Australians working in the oil patch of Southeast Asia.

His background had provided him with a fairly simple, straightforward view of the world: speak your mind and give everybody a "fair go." He couldn't have known the stark contrast Asia would pose to this mentality.

CHAPTER 3

Terry walked mechanically into the compact mess of the production facilities, made himself a cup of strong Indonesian coffee, *kopi tubruk,* and sat down at an empty table in order to think.

He had been with the project from the beginning and remembered Exacom's optimism at the outset. The prospect was centered between the mainland of Sumatra and a group of islands a kilometer or so off the coast in the Straits of Malacca. Padang and Tebing Tinggi Islands were the largest and closest of the group, containing a few fishing villages and dense jungles.

The discovery well had penetrated some ninety meters of light oil with a gas cap of about ten meters. It flowed a peak of eleven thousand barrels of oil a day from the best zone with little pressure drop, which meant that it was a very good well. The field was subsequently found to be of fairly limited extent but was very worthwhile to develop. Five other wells were drilled to drain the reservoir effectively, and all were hooked up to a production facility constructed on the Sumatran mainland. From there, the oil was pumped to the port of Dumai, where it was loaded into large tankers bound for Japan.

Under the profit-sharing scheme of the Indonesian government, once the development costs were recouped, eighty percent of the profits went to Pratama, the state-owned oil company, and twenty percent to Exacom. Nevertheless, at thirty dollars a barrel for a facility producing twenty thousand barrels a day, the return for Exacom was pretty good for the mid-eighties. The plans looked fine, but what happened during the development was a disastrous story; few things seemed to go smoothly. The worst part of it was the "haunted" water, home of Jin, the beast of these waters. According to the local people, he would strike at whatever caused him displeasure.

A number of diving companies had tried to do the routine seabed work during drilling and the pipe-laying work to connect the wells to the production facility. All had lost divers and had refused to operate further. One diver Terry talked with before he left claimed, "The water is too thick to call water, yet too thin to cultivate, and it sucks at you like a hungry leech even at slack water." None of the bodies could be recovered immediately, and when they finally were retrieved, they were in poor condition due to the current bumping and scraping them on submerged objects. There were two still missing. The cause of death in each case was determined to be drowning. Nothing more could be confirmed, yet the grotesque expressions on a few of the frozen faces suggested intense pain before death.

Only one locally based Indonesian diving company, Indive, was prepared to stay and was left to finish the project. The company had, in fact, connected all the piping joining the wells to the production base. It had also lost two divers but still persevered.

Indive's advantage was that it had established a base in Bengkalis, a nearby port, and trained local people. The locals were more familiar with the waters and the vagaries of Jin and used traditional wooden fishing boats. Wood, it was said, was more comfortable to Jin and would anger him less. To appease the monster, they would sacrifice a goat and enter the water through its spilled blood. Jin was supposed to absorb the life force from the poor animal, and while he was satiated, men could enter the water as long as they returned before the blood was fully diluted by the murky sea.

Terry thought of the way the expatriates had chuckled to themselves in the rig mess when Indive arrived on the scene and first performed the ritual.

"These people are full of goddamn superstitions," said the American drilling supervisor. "Why, they'd sacrifice a chicken before crossing the road!"

It had been easy to laugh then, but now it was a little grimmer. The Indonesians involved in the project indicated that the reason for all the problems in development was that Exacom had neglected to sacrifice an ox at the beginning of the project. When Padang #1 penetrated good oil, however, many Exacom people smiled smugly; it was only after that when the sinister rot began to set in.

Drilling equipment became stuck in the wells, and two bottom-hole drilling assemblies were lost completely, necessitating expensive re-drilling. The drilling rig used was a "jack-up" type, which contained the drilling and accommodation platform suspended between three large legs that were pushed down in order to jack the rig up over the sea surface into the drilling position. To move to another location, the legs were withdrawn, and the platform lowered until it was floating. The legs were then withdrawn further so the rig could be towed to the next location.

However, on four occasions, the legs could not be pulled from the channel bed. It was necessary to sink the rig as far as safety allowed and simply wait for the upward buoyancy to eventually pull the legs free from the suction of the mud.

The Exacom team had to wait three weeks for the rig to come free from the last well, and at a rig rate of seventy thousand dollars a day in the eighties, that was a rather expensive wait.

The rig itself broke down on two occasions, something that rarely happened elsewhere. Both problems appeared to have been caused by bad maintenance *or maybe deliberate negligence*, Terry thought wryly. The expatriate mechanic had been run off the rig after the last incident. He had shaken his head and cursed about the "grease monkey" he had working for him.

"He's so sharp at everything else," he grumbled. "Can't understand why he didn't grease the drum union. Bloody Indos, don't learn anything." Terry, however, thought that the expatriate fellow probably spent too much time playing cards while the Indonesian appeared to be running the shop.

Terry's own responsibility as a reservoir engineer was to supervise the testing of the wells. This involved flowing them under controlled conditions and taking measurements of pressures and production rates. The data recorded gave an idea of how well the well would flow when on commercial production.

None of the five testing operations had gone smoothly. There were leaking seals, damaged pipes, broken gauges, poorly calibrated sensors, lost tools, and human errors. Two different testing companies were tried; both turned in disappointing performances. By extrapolating, filling in lost data from experience, and making other assumptions, Terry felt that all the wells were very good, but he didn't have enough hard data to prove it beyond a doubt. Testing programs which should have taken a week had taken up to three weeks, and Exacom management became less keen to spend money waiting for more data.

So it went on, a six-month development program and sixty-million-dollar budget blown out to over twelve months and more than a hundred and fifty million dollars. Exacom's reputation had been badly dented as a result, which made quite a conversation topic around the bars of Jakarta, the booming capital city of Indonesia. The ultimate egg on the face, however, came when construction was finally completed, and the wells were turned on at the production base.

The official opening of the field occurred one clear morning before production started and was ceremoniously performed by General Siregar, the military head of East Sumatra, who had flown in specifically for that purpose. A ribbon was suspended across the entrance to the control room. A little dais was constructed, some food prepared, and the facility was made spotlessly clean. Indonesians thrive on ceremony, and the Indonesian workers were excited to see one of the top brass in the Indonesian military, particularly one they had heard so much about.

General Siregar had risen to great heights in a relatively short time after General Nasution's influence in Sumatra had declined. He was very active in developing the abundant resources of Sumatra. In Indonesia's "guided democracy," it was the military arm that did most of the guiding, and so it was very easy for a military head to take such a dominant role in the region's economic development. General Siregar's influence penetrated all the major resource development projects in Sumatra.

He was also rumored to have very sticky fingers and be active in the corruption that had unfortunately assumed a prominent role in Indonesian society at that time. The general's support for a project was a prerequisite for it going ahead and could be bought for a price, it was said.

His military helicopter had thundered down on to the helipad, and six Special Forces soldiers leaped out and gave the area a quick check. When the okay was given, General Siregar emerged and the Exacom Vice President, Ted Marsden, went forward to welcome him.

Siregar was tall for an Indonesian but carried some extra weight, normal for one with his status. He sported a large military moustache and had a hard, dark face, though his eyes were hidden behind tinted glasses. He exuded the impression of power commensurate with his position.

Terry had been asked to attend because he could speak fluent Indonesian and also because of the part he played in the project. He went forward with his boss and shook hands with the general, whose grip was surprisingly firm. "*Selamat datang,*" he began, the Indonesian welcome.

He then thanked the general for honoring Exacom with his presence and invited him to open the facility by cutting the ribbon. The general politely said that he would be delighted and allowed himself to be led to an ornamental chair on the dais next to the vice president. Ted then gave a short speech in English, again saying how honored Exacom was to have the general open this production facility and that it was Exacom's wish that such a project would benefit everybody involved.

It was then General Siregar's turn to speak. His voice was clear and strong, and he spoke in good English.

"Thank you for your nice speech, Mr. Marsden. It is my own pleasure to be here. I like to be actively involved in developing Sumatra's resources. This project is part of our aim to utilize our natural resources as quickly as possible so that our country can enter the elite group of developed countries. It is a small step toward securing a better life for our future generations.

"We acknowledge that Exacom has done a great job in developing what has proved to be a very difficult field. We all know that Indonesia is still very new to modern technology and management methods, so we still need the help of companies like Exacom to get us started. We have also heard that many problems were encountered throughout the development of the Padang field here. I wonder how many of these could have been avoided if the ancient customs had been followed." He paused for effect. "Perhaps both sides can learn from each other." He continued with a broad smile on his face.

He then switched to Indonesian and directed his comments at the Indonesians working on the project. He told them that they should be proud to be involved in taking a step further toward Indonesia's energy self-reliance and that they should learn as much as possible from Exacom and work hard to use what they learn for the benefit of everybody. He wanted Indonesians to earn a reputation as hard and capable workers.

Ceremony, polite conversation, and stirring speeches are part of the Indonesian way. It was true that some bosses were greedy and indulged heavily in corruption, but many others believed in the ideals they expounded to the workers. The people had very discerning eyes and realized who was bad and who was good. Terry wondered what they thought of General Siregar. He gazed at the faces of the listeners but couldn't find any clues there. The general's voice was powerful, and Terry had to admit that his heart seemed to be behind his words. Like President Sukarno, Indonesia's founding President, Siregar's oratory skills were quite compelling.

"So now I would like to declare the Padang field officially open for production," he said finally in English. He picked up the ceremonial scissors from the side of the dais and went forward to cut the ribbon. Everybody clapped, photographs were taken, and the Padang field was at last officially open.

Oil did not flow, however, for another two days. Due to all the delays, final checks and pressure-testing of the complex network of piping, valves, meters, and separators had not been completed. Terry was very busy during these last few days, double-checking diagrams, supervising the pressure tests, and completing last-minute details. When at last the time came, he turned on the wells one by one and anxiously surveyed the facility for signs of danger. A small leak and a spark could generate an inferno.

The nastiest surprise then hit him: none of the wells produced to expectation. He felt that each should realize at least five thousand barrels of oil a day in production conditions, yet after waiting an hour for the wells to clean up and stabilize, the best could only manage less than half that at the ideal production pressure.

That's odd, he thought. He shut the wells in, and after a short delay, the wellhead pressures climbed to their proper values. There were, therefore, no leaks in the piping back to the wells. He opened all the valves again and once more checked the whole facility for leaks. The result was the same; the wells had been ruined somehow.

CHAPTER 4

⚓

Terry didn't relish reporting the poor production performance back to his bosses in Jakarta. From its former status as an Indonesian pearl, Padang oil field had become marginally economic. Exacom's response was very cold back in Jakarta, and even icier sentiment flowed back from the head office in the States when they were informed. Tersely worded faxes came in, demanding more information; Terry himself was summoned to speak via phone link to the vice president of production in Houston. He nervously recounted what happened, and silence followed his description and then a click and beep as the line was cut.

A tense mood pervaded the whole office. The expatriates would look away from each other in the corridors, jovial conversation was stifled, and people waited for orders to come from across the Pacific. All knew what the company was like when it was displeased with a section.

They were all liable to be replaced, like a previous office in the Philippines had been. In that case, due to cost overruns on a few dry exploration wells, the whole office, from drilling manager on down, had been demoted, released, or transferred back to the States.

So in Jakarta, the staff waited for the expected tough reaction from Houston. A few days passed, though, and nothing happened. Gradually the tension eased, the telex and fax machines hummed more frequently, and the whole office seemed to sigh in relief. A new well, Celedes, in Exacom's Kalimantan permit area, had passed through a large pay zone, and interest was being diverted to it. The results of logging were keenly anticipated, and most communications related to it.

Back in his Jakarta office, a month or so after he had returned from opening the production at Padang, Terry was tidying up some reports when Ted Marsden walked into his office. "How yer doin' there, Terry?" he started affably.

"Oh, not so bad, though still a bit concerned about job security," Terry replied.

"Yes, well, we're all feelin' that way, I guess. Even me. Though Celedes is good news. Say, how would you like to take some vacation now?"

This was not a good sign. Terry's mind jumped a mile forward. He was not yet due for a vacation, and to be offered it was a sign his future was being "considered."

"Oh, well, yes, but what about the testing on Celedes?"

"Don't worry about that. There's a new guy from the States coming over to look after it. Should be here on Wednesday."

It dawned on Terry that he was to be made the scapegoat. This was how many oil companies worked for a long time. Whenever a mistake or failure occurred, a head or two rolled. The particular heads may not have done wrong, but if they were close to the occurrence of the problem, their survival chances were reduced. Terry guessed he would be the one to get it this time, and after he was gone, life might return back to normal, but the problem was not necessarily fixed.

On the rigs, it was the same. There was a man, or "hand," a representative of a service company, for everything that needed to be done: to prepare the drilling mud, to measure the mud properties, to screw the casing together, to run the pressure gauges, to pump the cement, to run the wireline logs, and so on for the many different activities necessary to drill an oil well. If a problem occurred, and time was lost or money wasted (usually both), the man responsible was "run off" and replaced. The man himself may have been the best at his job, but somebody had to be sacrificed to solve the problem, according to the established practice.

Terry mused that perhaps the difference with Indonesians was that they made their sacrifices before the work commenced and, thus, before the problem occurred.

"Yeah, okay," Terry began, setting his thoughts straight; he was not amused. "When and how long?"

"Let's say, from tomorrow," replied Ted. "Leave a set of notes so we can continue on what you've been doing and to give the new guy a good start. Andrew Sibley, I think, is his name. You've kept pretty good documentation of what's been done up there in Sumatra; that shouldn't be a problem. For how long? Er… let's say a couple of weeks. We'll let you know. No problem?" He avoided Terry's eyes and gave a half-hearted smile.

"I see," replied Terry coldly, his face now dark and empty of expression. "No problems. I should be able to handle it." His pride forbade him from showing fear or subservience.

"Okay then," said Ted finally, obviously a little uncomfortable with Terry's direct and cold reaction. He turned and walked out.

So, thought Terry, *I'm to be the run-off son of a bitch*. He couldn't believe it after seven years of reliable service. *I'm in the wrong situation at the wrong time*, he told himself, *as simple as that*.

After this little shadow play from the boss, he now expected to be put on vacation and asked to resign when he returned. Alternatively, he might be advised that his next assignment was to count the weekly consumption of ballpoint pens in Timbuktu, something he would not accept. Some intuitive feeling Terry was beginning to have about Ted, however, was making the first case look more likely. Those averted eyes and body language hinted at the worst. If Terry's nationality had been American, he thought, he might have survived, as Exacom's culture at that time was very much an American old-boys' network. Production was falling in Australia, and Australians were not required as much as they had been in the past.

The rest of the day, he spent tidying up his office, transferring a few personal items into a box to take with him and writing some changeover notes. Bad news travels fast, and it wasn't too long before his closest work colleagues started coming into his office to offer support.

"Bugger."

"Still, it might not be too bad. They've only asked you to go on vacation. Anything might happen while you're away."

"Yeah, but I'm not going to get my hopes up."

"We'll put in a good word for you."

"Thanks, guys, I appreciate it."

"It isn't over till the fat lady sings."

"I reckon she's singin' now."

"Just take some time out and enjoy yourself."

"Thanks, mate, I think I will."

The other office staff were friendly enough and carried on as usual. Today he was here; tomorrow he would be gone. The suddenness was part of the plan; the other expatriates would understand what happened, breathe a sigh of relief it wasn't them, and again be reminded that Exacom was a performance-oriented company; no position was sacred.

He left the office as the setting sun bathed the western sky in orange. The moist tropical atmosphere and the Jakarta smog made for superb sunsets; the whole Western Hemisphere was glowing orange. Jakarta was teeming with life, as usual. After the neutral air-conditioned office, his senses were assaulted by the city. The warm, sticky air was full of the numerous smells that made the city. There were delicious aromas from the little food trolleys cooking fried noodles, fried rice, satay, and soup. Then there were the more unpleasant smells, like car fumes and the stench of stagnant water in the surrounding canals.

Outside of the parking enclosure, cars hooted and growled; the horn was the most-used accessory on any vehicle. People yelled out, and whistles shrilled from traffic policemen and the little men who helped park cars for a small fee. The complex fabric of life flowed and ebbed, always in motion, permeating all the senses. Terry contemplated what a fascinating place Jakarta was. All this humanity, some nine million people, participating in a crazy race where, for most, the prize was to simply exist. Every day on his way home from work, he would see something different, something that would surprise him. He loved it, and it made him feel optimistic. If these people could live like that and still smile and joke as they did, he had nothing to complain about.

He lived in the Exacom housing complex with Lestari, his Indonesian wife. It was only five kilometers away but a good three-quarters of an hour in the normal Jakarta traffic. This day was no exception: bumper-to-bumper, no lanes whatsoever, vehicles jostling like a herd of impatient animals from one set of traffic lights to the next.

The first time Terry had been driven in Jakarta, he was simply amazed how one could get from point A to point B unscathed. It was about a month before he had the feel of it and trusted himself behind the wheel of a car. There was a system that you had to learn, and, once mastered, driving was not much of a problem.

Nevertheless, Terry still preferred to use a driver. It was simply not worth the aggravation of driving yourself. Fortunately, Exacom provided both a car and a driver, Abdul, who turned out to be a real gem. Terry caught up on a lot of reading while Abdul calmly negotiated the traffic jams, the floods, the road repairs, the *becaks*, the suicidal pedestrians, and the insane bus drivers. Abdul's monthly salary was about the same as what Terry would spend going out with Lestari for a meal in one of the nice hotels in Jakarta. Nevertheless, for all his efforts, as the driver of an expatriate, Abdul considered himself well paid.

Terry's daily surprise on that evening was seeing a becak careen into a canal as it tried to negotiate an intersection after the light turned red. It had gathered a good head of speed and was on a collision course with a bus to its left. The poor driver swerved to his right and charged straight into the adjacent canal. His unfortunate passenger, a well-dressed Indonesian man, probably a clerk, made a jump for it and found himself waist-deep in foul-smelling mud. The becak driver was worse off, as he landed on his stomach and for a moment disappeared completely from view into the rank slime. He scrambled to his feet looking like a wet clay doll, blinking as his brain attempted to sort out the sensory overload.

A crowd quickly gathered, and when they saw that nobody was hurt, a seed of mirth spread through the people like fire. Soon everybody was hooting with laughter, except the poor old becak driver, who was still immobile in his bewilderment, and the clerk, who was trying to gingerly pick his way to where his briefcase had disappeared. The laughter was infectious and spread to the people waiting in their cars and beyond as others joined in, laughing at

28

the people laughing. Terry doubled up and was almost in tears, while the becak driver was still trying to pull it all together.

Then beep, beep, beep—the lights turned green, and the traffic on his side started easing forward. Abdul, who was concentrating on the traffic and did not notice the misfortune, eased out the clutch and crossed the intersection, leaving the bubble of mirth behind. From the rear window, the last thing Terry saw was that the clerk had retrieved his case and was making his way to one side of the canal to climb out. The becak driver was still staring up at the crowd, his mouth agape, like a creature risen from the mud.

The brief moment of misfortune and shared mirth was swallowed, and Jakarta moved on.

As he approached the entrance of the complex and reached for his identity pass, Terry wondered how Lestari would take the news. Fond recollections of his wife flashed through his mind. In his eyes, she was the classic Asian beauty: attractive, coy, and polite but with an underlying intelligence and a quiet strength. She had been a secretary for Exacom when Terry first arrived in Indonesia, and he became fascinated by her. He wasn't the only one attracted, though; she had quickly gained a legion of admirers. However, she politely refused all attempts of her expatriate admirers to be on more familiar terms with her and hid behind an aura of Asian mystery.

Jakarta had an abundance of other girls, and one by one, each available man took easier methods of satiating their desire for Far Eastern feminine charms. There were many single expatriate men in Jakarta in the eighties and more than enough places available to satisfy their urges. It became the standard macho thing to frequent one or two popular bars in the evening and brag about one's nocturnal conquests the next day.

"I tell you, this town is somethin' else," Terry remembered

a new geologist saying. "Before I came here, I said there was no way I was going to take a whore. But after two weeks on the rig, you come back and go to the Oasis for a beer. That beer's good and so is the music, after the throbbing of the rig's diesels for fourteen days. A man feels relieved, and then a cute little girl wanders up with a big smile, snuggles close, and asks if you would like to buy her a drink. 'Sure, honey, why not.' So you do a bit of dancing and 'Hey, why don't you come home with me tonight?' So she does, and in the morning, you slip some money into her handbag or shoe, pay for her taxi home, and she gives you a nice big smiling thank-you. Is that whoring? Hell, no. That's just fucking excellent!"

Then some stud would get a dose of venereal disease, and things would cool off for a while. "Who was it?" "Where was she from?" all the others would ask. A trip to the medical center and the whole office knew what the problem was, even the secretaries. *Or especially the secretaries*, Terry thought. There wasn't much they didn't know. He had seen them exchanging knowing glances with each other when the "patient" had returned from an ordeal at the doctor's office with a backside full of penicillin shots. The fellow would carry a bashful expression—"Sorry, boys, I ain't drinkin' tonight"—but in spite of this, the next night he was usually back to the normal routine. After detecting the disapproving attitude of the secretaries, Terry deliberately wound down his activity in the bar scene, correctly sensing that it was a barrier for more meaningful relationships with Indonesian women.

Terry had enjoyed the bars and their various entertainments when he first arrived in Jakarta. He was young and naïve and behaved like a little boy in a toy store. Many young expatriate men reacted the same way. For the most part, they had worked hard in relatively sober environments to get themselves into a position where they could achieve an overseas posting. Then they arrived in a place like Jakarta, and as their cultural norms melted away, they discovered a whole lot of freedom. Most tended to explore every new experience that they could find, with a great deal of zest.

Before the year was out, however, a feeling of emptiness began to bother Terry. Captured in the expatriate life he led at the time, he wasn't really connecting with the local people. What did the maids really think? What type of life had they experienced? What did a typical Indonesian family do in the evenings? He didn't know.

Terry started to bridge that gap by cultivating friendships with the Indonesian technical staff at work. Exacom was obliged by the Indonesian government to also employ a certain number of Indonesian professionals for each expatriate bought into the country. They came from local universities, and Exacom spent a large sum of money training them. The government's plan was to reduce the number of expatriate workers each year. The local staff spoke reasonable English, and Terry gradually started engaging them on matters not connected to the oil industry. He found them friendly and willing to talk about their country. They were less willing, however, to talk about their personal situations, and for a while, a barrier existed.

"Why don't you learn Bahasa Indonesian?" his closest Indonesian colleague, Rachmat, had asked one day as they gazed out the window, looking down on Jakarta through the haze. "You learn more about a country through its language."

"Not a bad idea," he had replied.

He contacted the Australian Embassy, which let him know of an evening course that its diplomats used. He started at the next available opportunity but found the teacher, an elderly male scholar from the University of Indonesia, to be the driest Indonesian he had ever met. He delivered his lessons by rote in the most soporific, monotone Terry had ever endured. The course consisted of three-hour sessions on Tuesday and Thursday nights every week. In the small town of Brewster, French had been the only language available, and Terry had skipped it to study biology. His brain was, therefore, not familiar with different languages, and he found it difficult to encourage it into embracing a new language. After the second week of lessons, skipping classes and joining the rest of the guys in the bars once more seemed a very attractive idea.

Then Lestari was employed as the secretary for the production department.

Terry was absolutely beguiled by her. She was tall for an Indonesian, and very attractive, with a slim body, high cheekbones, and flowing black hair. She had the most pleasant of scents as she whisked through the corridors of the office, and her dark-brown eyes sparkled but gave no hint of what she was thinking. She was a mystery, and she mesmerized Terry.

One by one, her other admirers gave up and returned their attention to the night time bar scene. Terry persisted and returned to his Bahasa Indonesian course with renewed purpose. He imagined that Lestari was delivering the course, and the old lecturer must have begun to wonder if Terry was gay the way he dreamily stared at him.

Initially, Terry concealed the fact that he was learning Indonesian. One morning, though, he decided that he would put his new language skills to the test.

"*Selamat pagi*," he said, beaming. "*Apa kabar?*" (Good morning, how are you?)

"Mr. Terry," she responded in English, "are you learning Bahasa Indonesian?" She smiled but was still all politeness and distance.

"*Ya, saya mencoba*," he replied. (Yes, I am trying.)

"*Kenapa?*" she responded. (Why?)

"Because if I learn Indonesian, I may win the heart of an Indonesian princess," he replied. Terry knew that this was very bold by Indonesian standards, but he had prized the words out of Rachmat and had been practicing them, so on that morning, he was ready to show off.

Lestari flushed, for the first time Terry had ever seen, and for a few seconds, her eyes released their guard, and Terry could see the amusement and softening within.

She smiled at him and replied in Indonesian, "I wish you success, but beware, your prize may be elusive or unobtainable."

At that, Terry was stumped. He couldn't quite work out her shade of meaning from all those words, but he gave her a big smile anyway and said, "*Terima kasih.*" (Thank you.) He returned to his office still smiling and floating over the carpet. He knew that he had touched her!

Like a slowly rolling snowball, their relationship started to gain momentum. Eventually, she accepted his offer to take her for lunch, which caused quite a stir at the office. The tempo increased from there. At first Terry feared that there would be a limit to how far he could get to know her, just like contact with his Indonesian work colleagues. He certainly had no plans for a long-term relationship, but as time passed by, the more endeared he became; she tantalized him. They talked, laughed, and joked, and every careless touch of her body sent his heart racing. The relationship blossomed a lot further than he had dared to hope.

CHAPTER 5

⚓

It was dark, and the overhead lights of the Exacom housing complex had been turned on. The security man recognized Terry and Abdul and opened the barrier so that they could drive through. They followed the main road, through the middle, a left, a quick right, and then he was home. The outside light was switched on, and his lovely wife opened the door.

"Hello, *sayang*," she said, beaming.

"G'day, gorgeous, how was your day?" he replied, taking her in his arms and kissing her gently.

"Good. How come you're late?" she asked.

"Oh, something at the office." He met her eyes. "Let's go inside, and we'll talk about it."

They fell together into a huge rattan chair in the living room, and he told her the situation. She looked at him thoughtfully with her deep brown intelligent eyes.

"So there it is, *sayang*. What do you think?" he finished.

"But they wouldn't get rid of you. You've worked hard for them for more than six years and have a good reputation."

"Yes, but I'm in the wrong place at the wrong time. You know how it is. Look at Perry."

"Yes, but he was useless."

"Okay, in his case they needed an excuse. What about Laurence, then?"

"Yes, you've got a point there."

"Anyway, I'm not too sure about Ted bloody Marsden. I can't explain it yet, but I reckon he might have more to do with it."

"Really? I felt funny about him too when I was there," she said. "He used to eat me with his eyes."

"With or without chili?" Terry quipped.

"Like this," she said and bit playfully into his chest.

"Yeow! Listen here, cheeky one…"

Then followed some mock wrestling until he manipulated her into a bear hug.

"Okay, okay," she said, panting. "Play's over, and dinner's ready."

"Kiss first."

"Okay."

She kissed him and then scrambled up to summon the maid to help serve the meal that had been prepared.

"Fatma!" she called, and the girl appeared out of her room to help Lestari put the food on the table. Lestari had asked her to be scarce when Terry came home, as she never quite knew what he would do to show his affection. It was the Indonesian custom that public shows of affection between husband and wife were frowned upon. Terry, her Aussie husband, was not as inhibited with his actions and was likely to cuddle and kiss her as the urge came upon him, especially in their own house. Both the attention he paid her and the fact that it was different from her established norms excited her, though she still felt embarrassed when other Indonesians were present.

Expatriates, like anybody else who could afford it, were more or less obliged to have some hired domestic help. Foreigners who lived outside the company complex also employed a guard and often a gardener. These men were most likely connected in some way to the local community that the dwelling was situated in. If the home occupier chose not to support the system in this way, then theft of some sort or break-ins were inevitable. Lestari was used to maids and servants, and while Terry was away in the field, Fatma also provided some company.

"So, what do you think will happen?" Lestari began when they were seated.

"Oh, I'll probably be asked to resign while I'm on vacation, or maybe I'll be advised that I'm to be transferred to the Sahara as a sand-quality surveyor."

"Don't be so pessimistic. Maybe they just want a while to think about it."

"We'll see. We're allowed to stay here until a decision is made."

"Well, don't worry about it, my love. I think you're wonderful, and I love you so much."

Terry looked at her lovely, sincere expression of support and was again grateful for the fortune that had bought them together as husband and wife.

In the early days of Terry and Lestari's courtship, her parents were not pleased that their youngest daughter was interested in an *orang bule* (a white man) and made it difficult for Terry to take Lestari out.

It was not that To'ar and Niar Pantou were mean or ignorant—quite the contrary, in fact. They were simply concerned about the welfare of their daughter. Even though Lestari was twenty years old, she had still lived at home with her parents, as was the custom. Traditionally, they would look after her until she was married. To Terry, they were very polite and smiled nicely but would ask for Lestari to be home at nine thirty on a Friday evening, even though it was not possible to leave the house by eight o'clock. This did not permit long, pleasant evenings together. Lestari, to Terry's surprise, then suggested they should sneak around a bit. At her suggestion, he would park on a corner, and she would arrive in a becak after telling her family she was going to a party with her girlfriends. Then they would go to a restaurant, see a movie, or do some other innocuous activity just to be together. It was all so sweet and innocent that Terry sometimes felt like a twelve-year-old with a hopeless case of puppy love.

After a few months, they found themselves one night, after an excellent meal, on the grounds of a hotel overlooking Jakarta harbor. The moon was full, the waves murmured softly on the beach, and Terry took her gently in his arms. He looked into her dark, sparkling eyes and moved closer to kiss her. She did not resist, and the emotions released were almost solid enough to grasp. For Terry, the whole build-up had been like a fairy tale, and the magic he felt when he held her that first time was sensational.

From that point on, the relationship became more intense. Perhaps it was the elaborate way they arranged their meetings, perhaps it was the yearning for each other in the evenings when they were apart, perhaps it was the excitement of a completely different experience for them both and the unknown ahead, or perhaps it was the growing understanding of each other that they were developing. After twelve months of courting, they both felt that they had covered a lot of difficult ground with a very special person.

Terry had read somewhere that real love between two people develops like trees intertwining their roots underground. Two trees, initially separate, become one. Terry realized that their roots had become intertwined, and he couldn't untangle them, nor did he want to. He wondered whether Lestari's family and traditions would be a barrier to developing their bond further.

Although he thought he had come to know Lestari quite well, he was unsure of the hold her culture had on her. Somewhere in the emotional frenzy, he realized he was in love and asked her to marry him, and, to his surprise, she was willing. Then came the tricky bit: breaking the news to her family and winning their approval.

Lestari knew her parents had an idea something was going on. There was a situation that occurred one night after she returned home from meeting Terry and found his wallet in her handbag; he had given it to her for safekeeping at a dance place they had tried. She looked at it aghast. Terry, meanwhile, had discovered its loss and was puzzled what to do, as he was scheduled to fly out of Jakarta the next morning on a field visit to Padang. He couldn't go up to the front door and ask for it back, so he wrote a note on a piece of paper and gave a couple thousand rupiah to a becak driver to deliver it to her, making out that it was a note from a friend. Lestari came to the door when the becak driver knocked, but, of course, her mother and father were in the living room. Eventually, she came out with the wallet but not without leaving her parents feeling uneasy that something was happening to her. No Indonesian friend would get a becak driver to deliver a message!

One typically hazy, humid evening, Terry drove directly to the Pantou house. Lestari's parents were surprised to see him again, though in their Indonesian way, they smiled and invited him to sit down for a cup of sweet tea. After civilities were exchanged, Lestari came straight to the point and explained what had been happening and how deeply in love she and Terry were. Terry then formally asked her father—Pop, as he called him—for his daughter's hand in marriage. Pop's response was cool, but his poor wife burst into tears. Terry could understand why she was so upset: her daughter wanted to walk away with a foreigner.

"Well," Pop began, "this is a very big surprise for us. I'm afraid this will take a long time to think about. You see, this is Indonesia, and the whole family must be informed. I mean my brothers, sisters, and elders, and the same for my wife's side. You must let us think about it."

Terry thanked Pop for his consideration and apologized for the surprise. He assured Pop that it was his dearest wish that they would get family approval.

They then waited. A week, and then two went by, and Terry was called to go offshore. When he returned, a month had passed, and then finally Lestari told him that the family would like to meet him the next Sunday evening. Lestari herself looked white and quite frail.

"What's been going on?" asked Terry.

"They've been putting the pressure on," she replied, lowering her eyes.

"What do you mean?"

"Well, asking me all the time whether this is what I want and have I considered this, and what about that, and because you're a foreigner, what happens if such and such. All the time they ask me. Everybody has come around, the aunts and uncles, all the same."

"Can you handle it?"

"Yes, but I get very upset and sometimes lock myself in my room, crying."

"What will they say on Sunday?"

"I...I don't know. I told them I'd run away if they said no."

"Jeez, that would have put a rocket under their bed!"

"Yes, they went very quiet after that."

It was a nervous Terry who parked outside the Pantou household on the appointed Sunday evening. He could hardly believe what he was doing, but his desire for a future with Lestari pulled him onward. Mom and Pop met him cordially and showed him to a seat in their small living room. Lestari was nowhere to be seen, which was a concern for Terry.

"The family has discussed this situation for a long time," Pop began once the pleasantries were completed. "And unfortunately we have to say no. We can't give our approval for you to marry our daughter."

Terry's heart sank, and his head began to spin. Then a strange thing happened. The spinning stopped, and the room became crystal clear; everything outside of the room vanished, and the passage of time seemed to slow. He saw Pop looking at him intently, his face still. Mom sat behind Pop, also immobile, watching Terry, her face quite tense. All was very quiet. Nobody moved for what seemed an eternity.

Suddenly, Terry's mind began racing again. His first reaction was anger. He had an impulse to leap up and storm out, cursing everybody and crashing back into his familiar Western world.

However, he controlled himself as he observed Mom's strained expression, and he realized what this meant for her. The daughter she loved wanted to go to a distant land with a foreign stranger. Terry's mother would have had the same feeling if an outsider had breezed into Brewster and announced that he wanted to marry one of her daughters. He looked back at Pop, who still had not moved and was watching Terry carefully with deep, quiet eyes.

The outer world slowly began filtering back to Terry; he again became aware of the noises on the street outside—the food sellers calling for customers and the rattling of becaks trundling by.

"I'm...I'm sorry..." Terry faltered, his eyes lowered. "I feel completely alone."

It was as though the whole world had become strange and remote; he felt far, far from home. His eyes moistened, though he battled to keep himself from falling over the edge into a lonely void of despair. After a few moments, however, he began to feel himself rally.

"Okay, fair enough. I can understand how you feel, but..." His voice trailed off. "I'm really feeling quite empty now."

Still, nobody moved, though tears had begun to well up in Mom's eyes and then make their way down her cheeks.

"Will the family let me see Lestari again?" he appealed, looking directly into Pop's eyes.

Terry heard the crash of a car door slamming and the sound of feet on the concrete walk outside. Lestari burst into the room. She had been kept away until that time by one of her uncles. He and Auntie had picked her up in the afternoon under the pretext of visiting a relative in the hospital. She was concerned about being back in time, but they politely refused to be rushed and stopped on the way back for some food, which infuriated her, but she could do nothing about it. It was considered to be very bad behavior in Indonesian culture to be angry at family elders.

Nevertheless, she started sobbing when she realized she would not make it back home in time for Terry's arrival. Her uncle and aunt were concerned and encouraged her to tell them what was bothering her. Between uncontrollable sobs, she told them that she wanted to be with the man she had fallen in love with and that it wasn't fair her family wanted to destroy her happiness.

42

Didn't they trust her? Uncle looked at Auntie. They exchanged understanding glances and nodded.

"Okay, Tari," he said. "We will take you home now."

Lestari's eyes were puffed up from crying when she entered the house, and tears still flowed from her eyes. She leaped toward Terry and hugged him, shaking and sobbing. Terry held her tight. His mind had stopped from the emotional overload. All he knew was that it felt good to have Lestari back in his arms.

A couple of cars started outside and moved off. He noticed people leaving the porch; they must have gathered there and remained silent through the whole affair.

After some minutes, Lestari's sobbing eased, and she shook less frequently.

"Have you been hurt?" asked Terry, concerned about what may have happened. She shook her head and buried it further into his chest.

"Okay then," said Pop eventually. "It looks like we have some talking to do."

In this way, the family had tested Lestari, Terry, and their feelings for each other. *Brother, what a test*, Terry reflected afterward. From complete and utter loneliness to fantastic jubilation, all in one evening. He was amazed they both had survived. He appreciated that it was a smart way for the family to find out how deep the relationship was between he and Lestari and whether they both had the strength of character to surmount the challenges of a cross-cultural marriage. Terry felt sorry for Lestari, who had been placed under the most pressure. Sometime afterward, he wondered what the effect would be if parents could do a similar thing in the West. He concluded that the rate of divorce would drop; couples couldn't go through that sort of ordeal if they didn't love each other absolutely.

It helped that Pop's family was originally from Manado in

North Sulawesi, and therefore Christian, while Mom's family was from Padang in Sumatra, and therefore Muslim. Their own love had surpassed a culture gap and endured all the challenges their different backgrounds had created. Therefore, they knew what it was like to adapt and compromise in order for love to blossom.

After this climax, the rest followed relatively easily. They talked frankly and at length about what was necessary to adapt to each other's culture. They discussed what was normally expected in Indonesia for a wedding and reached an understanding of the compromise they thought necessary between the Indonesian and Western cultures. The ceremony itself took just over a month to prepare and was a big event in the best Indonesian tradition.

Weddings in Indonesia are naturally large affairs. The main role of the wedding party is to declare to the whole community that the married couple are now man and wife and hence out of the courting game. Virtually everybody the bride and groom have ever known are invited. In addition, friends of the parents and other important people are also invited. It goes without saying that the extended family will be there. It would be usual for a family of Lestari's background to invite a couple of thousand people. These guests must be fed and entertained, so there was a multitude of things to organize, from booking a suitable venue to settling on the costumes of the traditional dancers who would perform.

It was a huge learning experience for Terry, as he had not been invited to an Indonesian wedding before. He thought it interesting that the first Indonesian wedding he would be going to was his own. Finally, all the details were taken care of, and Lestari and Terry were married in a fairy-tale wedding. They were both resplendent in traditional dress and fine style. Terry's family and a couple of his best friends flew to Jakarta for the occasion. It was a great day for Terry.

Terry couldn't suppress the gratitude, even now as he stared across his meal at his wife.

"What are you looking at, my love?" Lestari asked, coaxing Terry out of his reverie.

"A very, very beautiful girl," he said softly. "It was worth going through all we did to be here with you."

"For sure," she murmured, looking back into his eyes.

"Come on, let's go to the bedroom before we really give Fatma something to gossip about to her friends."

The morning sun streamed into the house. Within the perimeter of the compound, it was a fine, lazy morning. Those who had to work had gone long ago in a convoy of white cars to jostle their way through the traffic to their offices. Now it was peaceful behind the high stone walls. Gardeners sat on their haunches together, smoking their spitting, hissing clove cigarettes. The maids were gathered together at neighbors' houses, chatting away, probably about the strange ways of Westerners.

Terry had slept in and was indulging in the holiday luxury of a cup of traditional Indonesian coffee (*kopi tubruk*), some rich layer cake (*kue lapis*), and the *Kompas*, the local newspaper. There were English newspapers, but their coverage was limited compared to the Indonesian editions.

Interestingly enough, there was an article in the regional section about a new oil field, Melati, that was operated in Sumatra by Pratama, the state oil company. It was only about ten kilometers or so from Exacom's own Padang production facility. He read with interest that General Siregar had also flown in to open that production facility. The article related how he had congratulated the Pratama people on such quick development and said that it was a fine example for Indonesia to follow. Terry glanced through the article, looking for information about the quality of the field and the oil, not something normally found in a newspaper article, but in this case, there were a few facts toward the end. The paper claimed that, from only three wells, the field was producing eleven thousand barrels a day. The article even listed the API gravity of the oil, a measure of its quality.

"This is interesting, Tari," he called to his wife.

"What's that?" she replied.

"Pratama has opened a field near Padang that produces oil of the same type we are getting from Padang."

"Well, at least they're doing something right," she said.

"Yes, very right," Terry replied. "I hear there has only been a rig there for the last three months. They've moved very quickly."

"Do you think Indonesians are so stupid?" she chided. "If Exacom found so much oil up there, then for sure there's more oil around, and that's where Pratama will look." Then she switched to her local dialect to chide him further. "This silly man must think we're a bit simple, my goodness!"

Terry laughed and went to give her a big hug. "Sorry, sorry, Your Highness. I am silly, and you are right," he joked. She brushed him off.

When he returned to his coffee, however, his eyes became glazed as the seeds of an idea spread through his mind.

"Tari," he called again.

"What is it this time, *sayang*?"

"I think I might go to the Mine of Information tonight."

"Oh no, you don't!" she warned.

The Mine of Information was what Terry called the most

well known bar among expatriates in Jakarta at that time. Its official name was the Tarakan Bar, and Lestari didn't like Terry going there at all. Even mentioning the place displeased her, which was why Terry invented his alternative name. Most of the expatriate oilfield men in Jakarta who were single (and even those who were not so single) ended up there for some part of Friday or Saturday night. Stories were swapped, acquaintances renewed, and oilfield gossip caught up with. If a fellow had been in the field for some weeks, he could roll up at the Tarakan and get up-to-date within a few hours. He could also drink his fill (or more) of cold beer, stagger around the disco floor for a while, and leave with a nice, warm girl.

It was the latter that Lestari objected to most vehemently. She felt disgusted by the girls in the bar who made money exploiting the basest of male desires. Indonesian society was entrenched in tradition, and a "respectable" girl kept herself for one man only. A woman's virtue was valued highly, and, rightly or wrongly, to lose it was to lose respect. It was one of life's tests for a woman to preserve sexual activity for her eventual husband, and in so doing, she gained strength as an individual through the self discipline it required.

Lestari didn't believe that girls were forced into bars by economic circumstance. As far as she was concerned, all girls had a choice, and bar girls had chosen the easy road. Lestari had been through tough times herself in her childhood, and she certainly had seen a lot of women who were a lot worse off but did not surrender to the attraction of easy money earned at the bars. She also acknowledged that there was a double standard between men and women. If anything, Indonesian men gained status through sexual conquests before marriage, whereas women lost everything. She didn't like the situation but accepted it, choosing to focus on the benefits her culture provided for her. She held with contempt all those women who profited from sex outside of marriage.

"I've got an idea," Terry said, consoling her. "I'll tell you about it soon enough, but I need to find out a few things first."

Lestari's face clearly showed her disapproval.

CHAPTER 6

⚓

The Tarakan never changed, Terry thought, as he looked around from the bar. The lights were dim, the music was loud, and the half-pints of beer were cold and superb. Memories returned from pre-Lestari days when he had enjoyed the sustenance available from this drinking hole.

He had arrived at about ten o'clock in the evening, which was still early for the Tarakan, and the place was by no means crowded. The disc jockey, in his glass enclosure upstairs, was choosing the best music. A few girls were there already, and a number of other expatriates sat around the central bar. Terry reminded himself that he should go easy on the beer if he wanted to get through the night. However, it always seemed to taste better in that place.

"You want to buy me a drink, mister?" came a voice to his right. He looked around to see a pert Indonesian girl looking up at him with inquiring eyes.

"No, thanks," he replied in Indonesian. "I'm waiting for a friend."

"You speak Indonesian?" she said.

"A little," replied Terry.

"*Bagus*," she said, putting her thumb up in approval. "Very good, mister." Sensing that "mister" was not interested in her, however, she drifted off.

"Hey, Terry, how's it goin', guy?" Terry turned to see two

Exacom staff members, Jim and Barry, the confirmed bachelors of the office, walking toward him from the entrance.

"Not so bad," he replied, smiling. "I knew I'd have to bump into you two. Let me buy you a drink." He motioned to Mamasan, the huge bar lady.

"So, what are you doin' here?" asked Jim. "Let me guess. You've had the first bust-up with your old lady."

"She kicked you out, has she?" teased Barry.

"No, I got a pass for tonight," Terry replied, and to encourage them, he added, "A fellow needs some fresh air once in a while."

"With us, lad, it's always fresh!" returned Jim. "This 'getting hitched' business is for old people!"

"Well, I'm doin' all right," answered Terry.

"And that's why you're here?" asked Barry.

"It's the best place I know for catching up on oilfield gossip," countered Terry.

"That's true," said Jim. "So what's your story, then? Marsden seems to have it in for you."

"Is that right?" asked Terry. "I thought it seemed like I'm to be the latest sacrifice."

"More than that. The son of a bitch has blamed you for the lot. He says that Padang was never as good as we thought, that not enough data was collected, and what stuff we got was not interpreted correctly!"

Terry stared back at Jim, and it was a while before he said, "That's incredible."

"Sure is," said Barry. "But he's the boss, and Houston is very agitated, so everybody's gotta wear it."

"Oh well," sighed Terry. "Such are the workings of a big oil company."

"Anyway, man," offered Barry, "with your background,

you'll have no problem finding another job. I hear that Conoco's hiring."

"I haven't even thought about it, to tell you the truth," replied Terry. "I guess it will be a bit strange to be out of work for a while."

"Jeez, look at that!" interrupted Jim. "I haven't seen her before!"

"Where?" asked Barry, the conversation immediately forgotten.

"Over there, around the table on the left."

"Yeah, not too bad."

They had spotted an apparently new girl, who was more attractive than the usual; she was sitting at a table at the rear with other Indonesians, both men and women.

"Not for sale," advised Terry.

"They're all for sale!" responded Jim. "You've just got to get the price right."

"Well, I reckon that's more than you could pay," said Terry.

"Yes," said Barry. "I reckon you've gotta stick with what you're happy with."

"Well, isn't that marriage?" asked Terry.

"No, wise guy, I mean for screwin'," said Barry. "If you want to screw, you choose a girl you know who's clean and good fun, and after, that's it. You go your way, and she goes hers. There's no commitment, man, no hassle."

"Well, I won't argue," said Terry. "All I know is that this beer's good. Another one?"

"Sure, this is my buy," said Jim.

"Here's to the Tarakan and all who sail in her," called Jim when the Mamasan brought another round.

"Cheers," said the other two men.

"So, who're you with these days, Jim?" asked Terry.

"Oh, I've been takin' Suki home a fair bit," replied Jim.

"She won't let him look at anyone else," said Barry.

"You can't talk!" replied Jim. "I'd say Siti had you by the nuts. The trouble is, once you take one of them, then you get labeled as that girl's man, and the other girls aren't keen to go home with you at all. It's a funny sense of responsibility they have, but there you are. Anyway, Suki's good in bed, so I can't complain."

"I went down to the A Bar last week," said Barry. "I thought I'd try a change and took another nice young thing home. She wasn't much good, really, just lay there like a sack of potatoes, then farted, rolled over, and went to sleep when I finished. She even complained that I hadn't given her enough taxi money. Anyway, I don't know how, but Siti found out, and was she pissed off! What was I doing playing around with a village girl and risking catching the clap? I told her I took home who I liked, and then a real row started!"

"Yes, and you know he made up to her," said Jim, laughing.

"Well, I was horny again!" said Barry.

"And you knew damn well that the other girls wouldn't go with you," said Jim. "They called you a butterfly, and they don't like butterflies."

"And you guys reckon being married is more hassle?" said Terry, smiling. "I tell you, I'd much rather be married any day."

"Speak of the devils," said Barry, looking to the door. Two girls had just walked in together.

"Uh-oh, here comes trouble." Jim spotted them also and waved. The girls recognized the men and started making their way to them.

"*Selamat malam*, Jim. *Selamat malam*, Barry," said the first one, offering her right hand in Indonesian fashion. She was neatly dressed, though with thick makeup, and her partner was similar. "Who's your friend?"

"Hi, girls," said Jim. "This is Terry, and, Terry, you've probably guessed this is Suki and Siti."

"*Selamat malam*," said Terry.

"Are you gonna buy us thirsty girls a drink?" said Siti to Barry, batting her mascaraed eyelashes at him in a mock innocent sort of way.

"Sure," replied Barry, giving a knowing wink to Jim. "What will you have?"

"Two gin and tonics, please."

"Each?" asked Jim jokingly.

"No, no," said Siti, laughing. "One each will do, thank you."

They had already studied the place in detail. They had ascertained exactly who was there, whether they were being watched, and who was with whom, a cool assessment that took a couple of minutes. When they settled at the bar with their drinks, they began talking to each other quickly in their own dialect, sprinkled with a bit of Bahasa Indonesian. Terry couldn't understand much of it but gathered it was about the new group Jim and Barry had spotted earlier.

"So what have you two been up to?" asked Jim, interrupting their conversation.

"Nothing much," replied Siti, obviously the more confident of the two.

"What a life, ay? Of nothing much," teased Barry.

"I still study," volunteered Suki. "But my mother now is sick, so I must look after her."

"Hey, this is a good song," said Siti, probably wanting to change the subject. "Are you gonna dance with me, Barry?"

"Okay, why not? I could burn a few calories. Are you comin', Terry?"

"No, I'll stay here, thanks," replied Terry. He didn't feel like dancing without Lestari. The difference between her and these girls was a whole universe. Now, he realized, this place actually helped him to appreciate his wife even more.

The tempo of the night increased with time, the bar became quite crowded, and the air grew smokier. The large speakers thrashed out the most current music, and a number of people began dancing, illuminated in colors under the flashing lights. Terry watched Jim, Barry, and the girls dance for a while. The men were carrying a few extra kilos, thanks to good living as expatriates in Jakarta, and looked a little clumsy. The girls, by contrast, had a natural rhythm and looked good, though they certainly danced to be looked at.

Terry then recognized a group of fellows farther around the bar, who he knew worked for Schlumberger, a large oilfield service company that performed electrical surveys in oil wells. He picked out an engineer who had been involved with the Padang field development and went over to join the group.

"Hey, Chris, how's it goin'?"

"Oh, Terry, not so bad now, for sure." Chris was from England and in his mid-twenties like Terry. He was an easygoing, approachable person. "I'm extremely glad to be back in town," he said.

"They've been messing you around, then?" asked Terry.

"Yes, like they always do. We're short of engineers as usual, so I've just come in from three weeks straight," answered Chris.

"Where were you?"

"South China Sea, Esso's new project."

"Haven't done anything in Sumatra, have you?"

"No, not since Padang. Are you going to drill more wells there?"

54

"Not as far as I know, but then again, I won't be working for Exacom anymore."

"No kidding! What happened?"

"Oh, I think I've been given the boot over Padang's poor production."

"Gosh, and I thought service companies were bad. Well, old boy, get plastered like I'm going to do tonight. Forget about it all. This beer goes to the head quickly after so long on a dry rig. I've only been here an hour, and I want to go to bed with all these gorgeous sweeties."

"You don't know who logged the Pratama wells near Padang, do you?" asked Terry. "Sorry to ask before your journey into paradise."

"No, I've been in the netherworld for so long, I'm not in touch anymore," replied Chris. "Though we've got a couple of land bases over there. Pierre over there would know; he works in Sumatra. Pierre!" he shouted to another fellow in the group of half a dozen. Pierre was French and sported a bushy handlebar moustache.

"This is Terry, he used to work for Exacom," said Chris after taking Terry around to his friend.

"Hello, Pierre, how are you?" said Terry, offering his hand.

"Oh, not so bad. I get better as zer night goes on," he said, smiling. He was quieter than the others, preferring to listen to them talk rather than actively participate.

"Chris says you work in Sumatra," said Terry.

"I 'ope not for much longer. I want to get out of zat shitty place."

"You don't know who logged those Pratama wells near the Padang field?" asked Terry.

"Er…yes, zat was done wiz zer truck from zer Asamera base. Zere was only a few wells. Zer crew drove down."

"Who was the guy?"

"Oh, a crazy Canadian fellow, 'e is called Andy 'Erbert."

"Andy Herbert?"

"Yes, do you know 'im?"

"No, can't say I do."

"He's drunk most of zer time. I don't know 'ow 'e does a logging job, but 'e gets on well wiz zer Canadians from Asamera."

"Still up there, is he?"

"Yes, but only for a mons or so more, as Asamera is closing down operations in Indonesia. Probably 'e vill quit after zat or be asked to quit."

"Didn't see the logs from those wells, did you?"

"No, in fact, zey were tight holes, which is surprising for Pratama. Zey would not even let us keep copies for our files. I remember zat because it is quite unusual."

"The wells must have been good, judging from production figures."

"So zer story goes. Zey must 'ave been lucky."

"How do I get to the Asamera base, then?"

"You must be crazy! Sumatra is a shitty place to work, and you want to go zere?"

"Well, yes," replied Terry, laughing. "I'm into shitty places and like to travel off the normal tourist track."

"Well, everyone 'as 'is own sing, I suppose. You've been to Pekanbaru?"

"Yes, of course. We used to crew change there on the way to Padang."

Pierre described the way from there. "Zey 'ave some security on zer base, but zere are so many expats, it is no problem to get in. Say you are new from Schlumberger and want to find Andy 'Erbert. Look at zat wanker!"

Terry turned to see who Pierre was referring to. A fat

56

oaf of a man was stumbling around the dance floor in his own drunken pleasure, oblivious to who he was knocking into. He was the epitome of "oilfield trash," with a cowboy hat, leather dress-riding boots, Levi's jeans, and a denim shirt with checkered inserts on the shoulders unbuttoned to just above his navel. His sleeves were turned back to reveal tattoos on hairy arms above the wrists, which sported a thick gold chain on one and a Rolex on the other. He wore another gold chain around his neck and a number of large rings on his fingers.

"That chaps," Terry heard Chris say, "is an embarrassment to our humble industry."

"Must be from the Deep South," another fellow said. "Coonass."

"Obviously hasn't been around here for long."

People were tolerating him, but Terry could see the bar staff casting a concerned eye in the exuberant fellow's direction and at each other. Trouble was usually dealt with swiftly here. Men would appear with an assortment of weapons and zero in on the problem very quickly.

Two other similarly dressed cowboys were sitting against the bar nearby. It appeared that they were in one group, probably overnighting in Jakarta on their way either to or from a rig. The fellow on the dance floor was with an ugly old maid, also very ample of body, with very thick makeup glistening under the gaudy disco lights. She was trying her best to smile as her partner staggered this way and that, groping every woman within reach. Finally, she sensed that he was going too far and tried to lead him off the floor, back to the bar. She had to grab one of his hairy arms and use subtle force so that he wouldn't explode in anger. With his other hand, he felt her breasts, backside, and inner leg while she did her best to deflect his groping and lead him to his friends. To her credit, the pair of them made it, and he sat on a stool near

Terry.

"Motherfucker, goddamn son of a bitch! Ain't this some place?" he shouted to his friends.

"Sure is," replied one. "Hey, Gerry, steady down a bit there; we don't want no trouble."

"Who's fuckin' makin' trouble? These assholes need our dollars, man. There ain't gonna be no trouble! Yee-ha!" he yelled at the top of his voice so that people nearby stopped their conversations and looked toward him. "I'm gonna go fuckin' tonight. C'mon here, bitch, let me feel your tits." He lurched at the old floozy, who was still with him. She dodged, and he knocked into Terry, sending his beer crashing to the floor in an explosion of splintering glass and liquid.

"Steady on, mate," Terry warned the cowboy.

At the sound of the shattering glass, everybody in the disco turned to watch the commotion.

The oversized gorilla took a few seconds to regain his balance and survey his handiwork. He then caught Terry's disparaging glare and took offense.

"The name's Brown, motherfucker!" he sneered, looking down at Terry. "From the tip of my toes to the top of my head, I'm Brown, and nobody fuckin' tells me to 'steady on.'"

Terry looked hard at the grizzled face. The man was obviously unaware of the disturbance he was causing and, in his inebriated state, was about as intelligent as the average gate post. Terry normally kept himself fairly well under control, but on this occasion, a spark of anger flickered within him. Perhaps it was a delayed reaction to his treatment by Exacom that caused some irrational belligerence to surface.

"Well, my name is Miles, and from the tip of my toes to the top of my head I'm Miles, except at my ass, where I'm brown," he said deliberately and loudly, locking eyes with his adversary.

"Motherfucker." The American swung a punch at Terry's face, but his size and alcoholic state did not make for lethal speed, so Terry was able to step back easily.

The fellow leaped forward like a wounded bull. Terry could not back up any farther because of the wooden fence around the dance floor nor could he dodge to the side because of the crowd. Both of them crashed through the fence and fell back onto the floor.

Terry's head cracked against the hard polished wood, and his mind exploded into sparks, and then a dark cloud dimmed his consciousness. He was vaguely aware of the American's face above him, puffy and red with animal rage, and of girls screaming. Then the expression of the oaf went dazed, and his body slumped beside Terry's. The fellow had been beaten over the head by a baseball bat wielded by one of the bouncers, who had materialized from nowhere.

Very quickly, hands dragged the limp body away and ejected it through a side door into the adjacent alleyway. The other cowboy-booted men were also herded outside by the growing army of bouncers and left to stand next to their friend's limp body, dumped unceremoniously on the moist earth in the alley.

The side door slammed shut, and Chris and his friends helped Terry up. His head was still throbbing, and he was dazed. When he reached up to rub his aching head, he could feel a huge lump growing on it and felt warm blood seeping from where the skin was broken.

"Here, clean up with this." Jim offered a clean handkerchief.

Terry tottered about unsteadily, and with time the spinning seemed to ease, though not the pain. He was aware of the disc jockey calming everybody down through the sound system and the staff sweeping up the glass and splintered wood and washing away the beer and blood. A well-dressed older Indonesian came into Terry's consciousness.

"Please, sir, you must go; we don't want any more trouble." He was probably the night manager and obviously very keen to return everything back to normal.

"Here, Terry, we'll drive you home," offered Barry. "You can't go anywhere with a knock like that. We'd better go to the hospital."

"No, no, it's okay," said Terry through his dizziness and pain. "Thank you. If you'll take me home, Lestari will fix me up."

"Okay, man. There's a medical center near the complex, anyway, if you change your mind."

It was well after two o'clock in the morning when they crunched to a stop at Terry's house. He rode in the rear while Barry and Siti took the front seats. Barry switched off the vehicle and walked around to help Terry, who was feeling a lot better, though he still had a throbbing headache. They had stopped at the medical center on their way. A doctor eventually arrived, cleaned Terry's wound, and administered an injection to combat infection. He also pulled a few pieces of glass from Terry's back, applied an antibiotic salve, and gave him some painkillers.

Terry clambered out of the car and knocked on the door.

"Lestari," he called softly. His wife opened the door quickly, as she had been waiting behind it until Terry identified himself. She stared in shock at the white bandaged head until she recognized her husband.

"*Sayang*, what happened?"

"Oh, I fell over; tell you about it later. Do you have any coffee? Barry and Siti have helped me for the last couple of hours," said Terry.

Lestari became aware of the other two people. She recognized Barry, but Terry felt her go slightly cold when she glanced at Siti.

"Yes, come in." She opened the door and, after closing it, went to the rear of the house to awaken Fatma, her long nightgown hissing over the marble floor. Normally she wouldn't bother disturbing the maid at this time, but she wanted to hear what had happened as soon as possible. She came back and fussed over Terry's bandages.

"Still hurt?"

"No, just a headache now."

"Want some painkillers?"

"No, the doctor has already given me something."

"Okay then, what really happened?" she asked, sitting next to him.

Terry briefly described the events of the night as she watched his face intently, gripping his forearm as she listened, deeply concerned. Terry finished the tale, and there was silence as Lestari digested it and looked at it from different angles. She then shifted it to the back of her mind and became the hostess again.

"More coffee, anyone?" she asked.

"No, thanks. In fact, I think we should be going. That was great," replied Barry. "C'mon, Siti."

Terry and Lestari saw the other couple to the door and waved them off. They locked and bolted the door and then retired to the bedroom. Lestari looked Terry in the eye and became very serious, the inevitable message leaping from her own fierce eyes.

"No more Tarakan!"

"I'm sorry, my love. That fight with the 'coonass' was my own silly fault." He touched her arm, looked back into her eyes, and smiled apologetically.

After the lights were out, she hugged him tightly out of

relief and to let him know she still loved him, but as she felt him become amorous, she pushed him away to the other side of the bed.

"What's wrong?" Terry asked, now sleepy with the drugs and aftershock.

"Not happy," she answered. *He would have to learn that he couldn't have it all his way*, she thought.

CHAPTER 7

⚓

"I'm not going!" Lestari declared defiantly.

"C'mon, Tari," Terry urged. "What's wrong with spending a week in Sumatra looking around?"

"But you want to sneak into the Asamera camp and 'look around'!"

"It will just be a matter of walking in. They'll think I'm an expat from a service company. Anyway, I know a guy up there, so it will be no problem. You can stay in the nearest town while I'm away; it will only take an afternoon to find out what I want."

She responded with silence and watched him pack his rucksack. They had traveled around most of Java together and had thoroughly enjoyed themselves. With their packs on their backs, they had taken the bus, walked, and hitched to many remote places off the tourist path.

At first, she was hesitant to adopt this European way of traveling; girls from her background used air-conditioned cars and good hotels. However, she soon forgot her inhibitions about traveling in such an apparently low-class sort of way when the fun of discovering the real magic of Java dawned upon her. The rural folk of Java were naturally friendly and greeted people who traveled modestly even more warmly. Moving about the country in a simple fashion opened up all sorts of doors. They were treated to a musical concert of traditional instruments, experienced perfect harmony listening to another village sing together, and witnessed faith healing and strange mystical feats in other parts of Java. Lestari had toured through Java as a girl but inside the metal and glass cage of a motorcar. She had never before witnessed the richness and warmth of the provincial Javanese.

She watched Terry pull the drawstring taut, tighten the straps, and then adjust the money belt around his waist. She couldn't stand the thought of being left out of something she now enjoyed. Compared to her friends, she had quite an adventurous spirit, which she attributed to her father.

"Wait!" she burst out as she dashed off to get her own smaller pack. "Somebody's got to come and look after you!"

Terry smiled to himself and watched his wife get her own gear organized. She would pretend to pout for some time, he knew, but then she would be good company and a pleasure to travel with.

Lestari still mystified Terry in some ways, but he realized that this was, in large part, because of the differences in their cultures that he had not yet discovered. Her serene demeanor when they were in mixed company was now less unfathomable, because he could detect the subtle changes in her face and body and had learned what they meant. The longer Terry knew Lestari, the less expressionless and fuller of character her face became.

When their backpacks were finally ready, they gave Fatma instructions and walked to the entrance of the housing compound to hail a taxi to the airport.

The dilapidated yellow taxi rattled up to the usual pack of cars waiting for the lights to change. The humidity was heavy from recent rains, and the roads slippery. Beside their taxi on the right was a well-dressed Indonesian man on a small motor scooter, and in front of him was another old, dirty yellow taxi. Terry looked around absently and watched the motorcyclist clean his glasses fastidiously and then inspect his smart clothing, flicking off stray particles.

The driver of the other taxi, meanwhile, decided to clean his windscreen and activated the squirters. Predictably, they were not aligned, so a graceful stream of water passed over the roof of the taxi and onto the motorcyclist, who was rubbing his glasses with a white handkerchief. He looked up at the sky worriedly and then at the wet droplets on his shirt with disgust. Again, the taxi driver used the squirters, and the water arced onto the gentleman's clean shirt and glasses, so he became more anxious and started rubbing his glasses with renewed vigor.

Terry's driver, unaware of this, decided to give his own windscreen a wash. The squirters were one of the few things working on this particular taxi, and a powerful jet of water erupted, not onto the windscreen, but neatly onto the poor motorcyclist. Better aim could not have been achieved with planning.

As the unfortunate motorcyclist alternated between drying his shirt and his glasses, Terry began chuckling. Another jet plopped onto his shirt, and then another from the first taxi, curving over its roof. The unfortunate fellow didn't know whether to continue rubbing his glasses or try to save his now damp shirt. He decided on neither and replaced the glasses on his nose and then took one hand and put his handkerchief on his head, glaring at the sky through the droplets on his glasses.

Lestari had now caught the action and was also snickering. As their driver released another spurt onto the fellow's shirt, they both burst into unrestrained laughter. The motorcyclist looked over at them uncomprehendingly, handkerchief and hand still on his head. Then the lights went green, and the traffic surged forward with horns blaring, leaving the fellow behind. Terry looked back to see him trying to restart his stalled motorbike while cars behind honked impatiently.

They managed to find seats on the midmorning flight to

Pekanbaru and then took a taxi into town to find the easiest way to Taklin, a smaller village only a kilometer or so from the Asamera base. Pekanbaru was a lot smaller than Jakarta but just as busy toward its center. All sorts of different people scurried about on their daily tasks while others smoked and watched them. The roads were rough and narrow so that their taxi crawled along with much honking and stopping. Bicycles stacked high with baskets or plastic wares, Sumatra-style pedicabs, horse-drawn carts, Pratama petrol tankers, and small scooters all vied with each other to make progress.

Storm clouds were gathering for the afternoon downpour when Terry and Lestari arrived in the town center, so they went inside a nearby restaurant to sit out the inevitable downpour and have a late lunch. They had not been sitting long before thunder rumbled from the sky ominously, and the first heavy droplets spattered the ground. People raced for cover as the heavens opened and a continuous sheet of water fell. Pedicab drivers pulled their plastic covers down and huddled inside their small cabs. The poor horses of the *bendi* (horse-drawn taxi carts) seemed to sag even more under the torrent, a forlorn sight while their masters waited under their cart awnings. A few trucks and cars still tried to use the street, their wipers useless in such conditions, and their wheels sent arcs of muddy water to each side. All roadside stalls had been packed away, leaving a few bare poles and frames. The street quickly turned into a river as water poured into drains barely able to cope with the deluge. Outside, activity temporarily halted, though under cover the pulse of life throbbed on, damp and smelly.

Sometime after eating, while Terry and Lestari were sipping their strong coffee, the downpour stopped as abruptly as it had begun. There was a short period of relative silence, and then the braver people stepped out from under cover, shortly followed by everybody else. The pedicab drivers pulled up their plastic covers and shook off the water from their vehicles, and within a heartbeat or so, life continued on as it had before the rain. Now, though, there were big puddles to negotiate, and mothers scolded their children for playing in them. Other children stood near puddles close to the road, so they were showered as passing vehicles splashed through.

"*Sudah?*" asked Terry. (Are you ready?)

"Okay, what now?" Lestari asked.

"Let's find a bus to Taklin," replied Terry, reaching for his pack. "Let's see if we can make it before dark."

The Mitsubishi Colt minibus, ever so popular in Indonesia during the eighties, rattled and bumped down the country road. Terry and Lestari squashed uncomfortably into a back seat, their feet on their packs and their knees near their nostrils. The driver shared the front bench seat sometimes with five other passengers. Swinging on the left-hand door hung the "conductor," half in and half out of the vehicle. It was his job to collect fares, find passengers, and yell out the bus's destination.

"Taklin! Taklin! Ayo, ayo!" he yelled at a group of people by the side of the road. One of the pedestrians waggled a finger, and the Colt clattered to a stop. A number of folk climbed in. One had a large basket of pineapples, which he threw up onto the roof. There was no such thing as too full. As long as folks needed a ride, they could be crammed in with whatever chickens or baskets they carried. If the bus became too empty, then they'd drive around the next village until it was more or less full again. Not for the first time, Terry thought, *this country is amazing*.

"Yo!" the conductor shouted to the driver, and they were off again. The amazing thing was that they would cover the hundred and sixty-odd kilometers to Taklin for a little more than a dollar. It could, however, be considered a small amount for the travel but not enough reward for the pain endured.

A small girl nearby smiled to her mother about the *bule*, or white man, in the bus. She looked at Terry, her white teeth shining in a big grin. Terry winked, and she laughed, cuddling closer to her mother. She then tried to wink but could only manage to close both her eyes. This time, Terry laughed, which made the little girl flush before trying again. Eventually, she mastered it and began winking at everybody else on the bus, occasionally looking back at Terry and smiling broadly to show how smart she was. This continued until her mother bundled her up and signaled the conductor to stop.

In their place, an old man climbed aboard wearing a *peci* (a black hat that Muslim men wear in Indonesia), white robe, and black-rimmed glasses. He held a walking stick. Terry smiled politely to him, and the fellow smiled back. He had few teeth left, and those remaining were nicotine-stained. Terry guessed that he was probably an older member of the local mosque traveling to another village to speak with the elders there.

Just as the sun was setting, they pulled up to the little bus depot at Taklin. Terry gradually straightened his legs and then tested them for weight; they were feeling pretty lifeless.

"My goodness, I'm glad it's no farther," sighed Lestari.

"At least your legs are okay. My long *bule* legs aren't made for these buses," answered Terry. Unsteadily, he eased himself out of the bus, supporting his weight on his arms, but then fell over on the ground when his legs refused to obey the commands of his brain. Many people looked and laughed, teeth and eyes flashing— he provided good entertainment. Lestari couldn't keep her face straight either. Terry gave in and burst out laughing himself;

his legs, however, remained asleep. Eventually, after strenuous rubbing, they painfully returned to life. He hobbled a little to wait for more circulation to return.

"I must look real funny," he commented to Lestari.

"Yes, dear, you do."

"Hell's teeth, another ten kilometers and I'd be a stretcher case."

"My poor husband," mocked Lestari, "who loves to travel like the locals do."

"Okay, okay, my cheeky wife. Where's the nearest hotel or *losmen* (cheap lodging)?"

It didn't take them long to find a modest hotel in the town one block back from the main street. They secured a clean room with its own bathroom and air-conditioning unit. There were other losmen in the town that had reasonable rooms available for about two dollars a night but with shared bathroom facilities. Lestari preferred her own bathroom if there was a choice and her expression when Terry suggested that they try the two-dollar establishments showed that she would not be reckoned with.

The town itself was probably a sleepy provincial backwater before the Asamera camp was established nearby. Numerous small stalls, called *warung*, for eating, drinking, and mostly talking the day away, lined the street, and a few restaurants obviously designed to cater to expatriates had been opened. Terry noticed a number of hardware shops and at least one billiards hall. He thought to himself that the inevitable houses of prostitutes and beer, common in oilfield towns the world over, would not be far away.

"Well, I'd better get after it," said Terry after they'd washed and settled in.

"You're kidding! It's getting late. Why can't you go tomorrow?"

"Because I'd like to chat with this guy over a beer, and I gather he doesn't get up too early. Besides, there are fewer people to see me in the evening."

"Humph! So I just hang around until you get back?"

"I'm sorry, dear, but you probably won't be allowed through the gate, and this fellow's a bit of a wild one, anyway. The quicker I find out some things, the quicker we can leave," Terry coaxed.

"Well, I'm going to go to the night market. And I might spend a lot of money!"

"Okay," Terry replied casually. He figured that it was not likely she could spend a fortune in a local market. "So what are you going to buy with a lot of money?" he asked, unable to resist the gentle challenge.

"You wait and see," she said defiantly, her eyes flashing.

"Well, ten dollars will buy a lot of bananas," he replied, smiling.

"Not bananas, silly, gold, and diamonds!"

"Here? In the middle of nowhere?"

"You had better believe it. Some of the best gold and diamonds come from Sumatra," she replied, smiling broadly back at him.

"Uh-oh. This could be expensive."

"It sure could, so you'd better not be too long!"

He gave her a hug and kiss, laughing at her sense of humor. (*She couldn't be serious*, he mused, but couldn't be sure). Still smiling, he let himself out and headed for the main street.

Outside, it was already quite dark, and the lamp lights in the little shops and *warungs* were flickering lazily. He paused at a local Padang restaurant to ask directions to the oil camp. It turned out to be straightforward enough, as in the evening, tiny minibuses, called *mikrolet*, left for the gates of the base every fifteen minutes or so. Terry clambered aboard one and before too long was bumping along a fairly large road to his destination.

The camp itself was behind a tall wire enclosure, its purpose to keep thieves from stealing useful bits and pieces from inside. There was a wide entrance with a guard's house on the left side. A couple of blue-uniformed guards lounged about inside while another casually stood outside, watching vehicles pass through.

The mikrolet stopped outside the compound in a turn-around area the size of a tennis court. Night stalls selling cheap clothes, trinkets, drinks, magazines, and a multitude of different foods surrounded the area. Each stall had a kerosene lamp that cast a bright flickering light over the wares inside. Stall owners chatted to each other and to groups of men who came out of the camp for an evening stroll. The surrounding land was flat and low lying; a littered canal passed behind this little microcosm of life and then flowed by the main road. The stall owners obviously used the canal to deposit all their waste.

Terry walked over to the guardhouse. "*Selamat malam,*" he said, greeting the fellow outside. "I'm looking for a friend called Andy Herbert, a Canadian. He works for a company called Schlumberger. Do you know where he lives?"

"Schlumberger, mister?" The man looked inside the little hut to his friends. The eldest guard had overheard the exchange and rose to come out.

"Where are you from?" he asked.

"I work for Exacom," Terry replied. "I'm on holiday."

The old guard seemed a little difficult, as though he relished his power and wanted to use it.

"Look, here's my Exacom ID," said Terry, showing the guard the plastic card in his wallet. The sight of something official seemed to do the trick, and the guard finally nodded and gave Terry directions.

"*Terima kasih*," Terry said, thanking him, and strode into the camp. On one side were the workshops, warehouses, and pipe storage areas of a typical oil camp. On the other, there were rows of neat, fabricated bungalows. It was in this direction that Terry headed.

Number 10-A was just like the others, with a small, neat garden and a short concrete driveway. Terry walked by the Toyota Land Cruiser parked outside and knocked on the door. There seemed to be light inside but no sound. He knocked again and waited. Still no sign of life. Just as he was about to knock a third time, he heard a shuffling in the room to his right. He knocked again anyway, and soon footsteps approached.

The lock rattled, and the door opened to reveal a bleary-eyed, hairy fellow clad only in a pair of underpants. He looked back at Terry, his frizzy blond hair and beard forming a bushy frame for his blinking eyes. All his prodigious hair was uncombed, and he looked like some wild hillbilly.

"Andy Herbert at your service," he said in his Canadian accent. "Who be you?"

"Terry Miles. I used to work for Exacom. I…er…thought I'd drop in. Hope I'm not disturbing anything."

"No, no. What time is it?"

"About seven o'clock."

"What day is it?"

"Saturday."

"Saturday!" He seemed quite surprised at first. "Oh yes, that'd be right. Damn, another day gone. I guess I should be getting up." He looked reflective, and then another thought crossed his mind. "Helluva way to come just to drop in, isn't it?"

"Yeah, well, it's information I'm after, really."

"Information? We have an information seeker then, do we? Well, you'd better c'mon inside." He turned around and strolled into the house, leaving Terry to follow. Andy turned on the lights to illuminate a very messy lounge room. It was sparsely furnished and even barer of decorations. Empty beer cans and bottles lay on the floor and most other level surfaces.

"Bless this mess," said Andy, waving around the room. "I've had a few rough nights." He turned around, scratching his hairy chest. His broad stomach hung over his underpants.

"Well, information seeker, what is it you want?"

"To see some well logs from Pratama's Melati field," replied Terry. "You see, I was the reservoir engineer involved with Padang. I'd like to compare it with Melati."

"Padang, ay? That was the 'super' field that barely farted when they got it producing."

"Yeah," said Terry. "Everybody must have heard about it."

"Well, I can't figure out how they got anything out of Melati. I logged the wells, and there seemed nothing at all down there. Mind you, they reckoned that the pay was in a fractured, cemented quartzose zone. That may be, but it didn't look too good on the logs. I would've said it was dry."

"Do you have the logs stored somewhere?" asked Terry.

"Not officially. We weren't allowed to keep 'em. Had to hand over the lot to Pratama and sign a paper saying we weren't to disclose anything to anybody."

"Bit strange, isn't it?"

"For Pratama, yes. Asamera, on the other hand, was sometimes into that, especially on wildcats. The old cloak and dagger works well for the share prices back home. The odd good rumor also works well for the company directors too. Naughty boy, Andy," he scolded himself in jest and smacked one of his hands with the other. "That's going too far. I'm not allowed to say things like that." It was a small jab at a few company directors who would "kite" their stock and profit by selling shares through a third party.

"Do you have anything left then?" asked Terry.

"Old Andy here is cleverer than that." He winked at Terry conspiratorially and tapped his nose with a finger. "I've got the odd tape and photocopies of the logs covering the pay on one of the wells. I have bursts of keenness every now and then and wanted, for my own interest, to have a closer look at this famous oil zone. I've got some good evaluation software I was going to use to see how much oil they really got. Never got around to it."

"Do you mind if I have a look?"

"What else do you want?" Andy teased. "My body?" And so saying, he thrust his arms in the air to each side and crossed his legs as though he were a crucifix.

"Well, what say I buy you a meal and a drink?" offered Terry.

"Ah, a man after my own heart. Just wait until I chuck some clothes on." He then disappeared into his bedroom, stepping over empty cans and bottles as he went. Terry looked around at the shambles, a typical bachelor hovel. Remains of food and alcohol were everywhere. Andy reappeared, thrusting his hairy head through a T-shirt and tucking his stomach into his jeans.

"The maids have this weekend off," he explained. "And I had a few of the remaining Asamera fellas over last night for a party. I can't remember too much about it, but by the looks of things, it went all right." He smiled at Terry.

"What's going to happen to the base?"

"Pratama is taking it over. There's only a bit of production going on. Asamera didn't have much luck here, and that's another story. In any case, Pratama wants to operate all the land permits in Indonesia and is pushing out the foreign companies. 'Scuse me," he said, moving past Terry to the door, where he slipped on a pair of old sandals. "Okay, let's get away."

"Where's your wheels?" he asked Terry when they were outside.

"I don't have any; had to bus it."

"A masochist also, ay? Hope I've got my keys…yes, there they are. Well, hop in," he said, unlocking the four-wheel-drive.

"You choose the place," said Terry.

"Not much good for you to choose it, is there?" teased Andy, his wild eyes twinkling in the night amidst his helmet of frizzy hair.

"Where're we headed, then?" asked Terry as they roared off. Andy was obviously not a defensive driver.

"There's a good place in town, great food, and cold beer."

"Maybe we can see some of that Melati stuff before we go?" suggested Terry. "I'm staying in town, anyway."

"Don't ask too much, do you?"

"Just a thought."

"Well, okay, won't take five minutes to dig out those old photocopies from the workshop."

They drove out of the residential area and into the industrial side of the compound. It was fairly well lit by overhead lights and contained assorted pieces of machinery among the workshops, a lot of it obviously rusting and forgotten. Andy drove through the silent collection of machine corpses and stopped in front of a large shed at the back of the camp, set aside from the main cluster of buildings a little way. "Schlumberger" was written in large lettering over the workshop entrance.

"Behold, our palace," said Andy.

Terry followed him to the gates, which Andy unlocked after fumbling awhile with his keys. Beyond the back fence and out across the paddy, Terry could see the signs of Asamara's one producing field. Flares burning off excess gas dotted the landscape like candles dancing in the night. Nearby was a particularly large one, illuminating the surroundings with a fiery orange glow. It was as though the flame was a demon frantically trying to break the bond that held it to the flare pipe. Desperately ducking and lunging to be free, it roared and wheezed a satanic dirge.

"Does it always smell of burning here?" asked Terry.

Andy was now fumbling with the chains. "C'mon, you bitch. Er...yes—got it!"

He opened one of the gates enough to let himself in.

"Shit!" he exclaimed.

Terry quickly followed, to find the place filled with a smoky haze.

"There's a goddamn fire here!" exclaimed Andy. "Quick, go to the guardhouse and tell 'em to get the firefighting unit. I'd better get the truck out."

Terry took the keys Andy gave him and flung open the double gates so that the survey truck could be taken out. He then leaped for the Land Cruiser and tore back through the compound to the front gate.

"Fire! Fire!" he yelled at the puzzled guards after skidding to a halt in front of the guardhouse. "At the back fence in the Schlumberger workshop! Get the fire unit!"

The guards looked for direction from the old fellow Terry had talked to on his way in. He took a couple of long seconds to respond. Seeing the urgency in Terry's face, however, he picked up his phone and dialed a number.

"Hello, control? Security here. There's a crazy foreigner here telling me that there's a fire at the back of the camp!"

Terry was exasperated at how slowly the fellow moved. It was as though he was discussing a recent movie with a friend.

"In the Schlumberger workshop!" urged Terry. "Hurry!"

He then jumped back into the vehicle, revved the engine, and dropped the clutch, spinning himself around in a hundred-

and-eighty-degree turn, calculated to convey the urgency of the situation. As he arrived back at the workshop, he was pleased to hear the alarm sound from inside the camp. The large survey truck had been driven out and was now idling some distance away. Smoke was pouring from the double doors, and flames could be seen through the windows of the office behind. Terry pulled up near the truck and looked around for Andy. Surely he didn't go back inside? As he was debating what to do, a muddy figure emerged between the burning building and the back fence. Terry rushed over to help him, but Andy waved him aside.

"I'm okay, man, just took a fall into the canal."

"How the hell did you manage that!"

"When I was climbing down from the truck, I saw some guys running away from the fence and across the fields. I ran around the back, where they seemed to be coming from, and caught another couple just passing through a hole in the fence. I chased 'em, man, without thinking, little bastards! Anyway, this footwear isn't the best for cross-country, and it's pretty damn muddy back there. So good old Andy slips, doesn't he? Straight into the mud! Son of a bitch, it's foul." His blond mop of hair and beard were dark with mud, and the whites of his eyes twinkled in the night; he looked like an ancient wild caveman. Terry had to suppress a smile as Andy went off cursing the "assholes" who burned his workshop.

The fire was well underway before an ancient fire truck rumbled down the road toward them. It swung around, and its crew jumped out, and like busy little ants, they made couplings and started the pumps. It was like watching an old silent Keystone Kops movie as they raced around screwing things together and then unscrewing them and trying something else, waving their arms frantically and shouting orders to everybody else. Someone figured the truck was too far away from the canal to pump water from, so they started it up again and tried to reverse to the fence.

This surprised a few crew members, who frantically tried to gather pipe and gear from the reversing wheels. Fortunately, the fire engine stalled before flattening too much gear, and when started again, the way was clear. All the figures dancing in the orange flickering light and smoke cast a bizarre scene, as if from a dimly remembered dream.

"Jesus!" cursed Andy. "Are these clowns going to put this fire out?"

With time, however, the boys became more organized, and soon a spume of water was spraying into the burning office.

A larger Land Cruiser roared up, containing four swarthy expatriates all sporting the peaked baseball-style cap typical of most oilfield workers. Terry guessed they were some of the remaining Canadian Asamera supervisors. They drew up near Andy and Terry.

"Got a problem?" began the driver, apparently the one with most authority. He then stopped dead and looked at Andy. "Jesus Christ! What happened to you?"

"I had an accident, I guess," answered Andy. "I was chasin' the motherfuckers who lit this goddamn fire!"

The other fellows alighted from their vehicle and came around. "Andy, old son, where've you been?"

Andy's white teeth shone as a smile broke. "Just takin' a swim, what d'you think?"

"You crazy son of a bitch!"

"Well, you'd better get washed up," said the older man. "You never know what you'll catch from this shit."

"I'll run you back," offered Terry.

"We'll look after things here," said the boss. "I don't think its goin' to spread, but looks like you've lost the office. The gear in the workshop might be okay, though."

"That was Mike, the supervisor here," said Andy as they drove away. "A real neat guy."

"And the other fellows?"

"We got Lou, Colin, and Bob—they're drilling guys. I've known them for a while now. They were around last night."

"So you reckon those fellas you chased might have started this?" asked Terry.

"Little bastards, I'd put money on it!"

"Why's that?"

"Oh, I had an argument and fired a guy last week. Lazy son of a bitch did nothing, yet he strode around the workshop like a peacock, ordering the younger guys around. I reckon he was the one. We have to get rid of some of our help anyway because we may have to pull out of here when Pratama moves in. If I see that bastard again, I'll kick his ass!"

They soon pulled up to Andy's "pad," and he went off to the bathroom to wash away the sludge sticking to his body.

"I'll make some coffee if I can find everything," offered Terry.

"Be my guest. You could be useful, after all," Andy said, smiling.

When they returned to the fire, a large crowd of people had gathered. The fire brigade had almost put the fire out and was still pumping dirty canal water into the smoldering building. The main workshop was fairly well preserved, albeit saturated, but the office behind was gutted. Andy honked through the onlookers and pulled up by the big survey truck he had saved from the fire.

"Better turn the old girl off and lock her up," he said, pointing to the truck.

Mike, resplendent in standard work boots, Levi's, and a lumberjack shirt, was over near the fire truck, telling the boys to ease off. The other Canadians were there with him, so Terry and Andy headed toward them.

"Hope you didn't have too much of value in the office," said Mike as they walked up.

"No, most stuff was in the safe, and that should be pretty right," said Andy. "Shall we have a barbecue?" The other fellows laughed at this.

"I guess you'll be barbecued when you tell your boss what happened," suggested Mike.

"Yeah, you know how they are with the electric debriefing chair. 'Why did you let your workshop burn down?' Had a friend who worked offshore, and the rig he worked on went down in a hurricane. Everybody was evacuated off it in time, but he had to explain in an accident report how he came to lose all his equipment."

"Well, I guess we can't do much here," said Mike. "I'll get security to stand guard, and you can salvage what's valuable tomorrow morning when it's all cooled down. By the way, who's your friend?"

"Oh yeah, this is Terry, the information seeker. He worked for Exacom and 'popped in,' to use his own words." Then, turning to Terry, he said, "And I guess the information you seek has gone up in smoke. Too bad, ay?"

Terry and Mike shook hands.

"Well, we were off to find something to eat in town," said Mike. "Why don't we all go together now? I'll get a few details from you while we're at it. I suppose I'll have to report this incident. I'll just get the boys organized."

After a short while, they were crammed into Mike's Land Cruiser and heading out of the camp. They found a brightly lit

Chinese place on the main road through town.

"We eat here a lot," Mike said to Terry when they had settled down. "Chinese food is pretty safe. There are other places in town, but they only seem to serve bits of things. You know, lungs, livers, hearts, brains, bats, and all that type of shit." Terry smiled at their comments. He guessed that sweet-and-sour pork would be the most-ordered dish and was vindicated. Except for Andy, of course, who tried to order tiger testicles. The young Chinese girl who took the order was a little confused.

"Tiger balls," explained Andy again. "You know—" He clenched his fists, put them between his legs, and roared like a tiger. The girl blushed, smiled politely, and averted her eyes while the other men burst into uncontrollable laughter.

"Goddamn," said Andy. "I thought the Chinese ate everything. What about elephant penis? That oughta feed us well." More laughter, and so it went until the poor girl disappeared for help. An older lady emerged shortly after and promptly informed the patrons in a no-nonsense way that if it wasn't on the menu, they didn't have it, so sorry. Andy finally settled for nothing more adventurous than chicken and almonds.

"Did I tell you of the craziest meal I had earlier this year?" Andy continued after the order had been taken. The others nodded their heads and rolled their eyes.

"More than a thousand times," Colin answered.

"You wouldn't want to hear about it," Colin advised Terry.

Andy wasn't to be deterred from retelling a good story, however, so he continued.

"My Indonesian helpers decided they would treat me one night. The fact that I was generous with their overtime may have had something to do with it, but I'd like to think that it was because I'm a great guy."

"Bullshit," interjected Lou.

"Anyway, I let them take me to a little restaurant some ways up the road from here. We were shown a room with a covered table high enough to sit at on small stools. We sat down and ordered drinks, a special wine they make from bamboo shoots. It was quite potent and relaxing, so we talked and mellowed out some. In the middle of the table was a large tin dome, like a food cover, and after a while, the staff brought out eating utensils and food like rice, vegetables, and sauces."

Andy paused for a long draught of beer.

"So I was starting to wonder what the main course was and when we would start. I was getting hungry. Finally, a weird-looking man in some sort of traditional costume appears, carrying a large machete. The other staff also gathered around. Before I was fully tuned in to what was going on, the food cover in the middle of the table was raised, and a round half-coconut-like hemisphere was revealed, protruding through the table. The joker with the machete makes a neat incision around the circumference and then, with one swift swipe, splits it open."

"Oh shit," groaned Mike. "Here we go."

Andy looked at Terry. "You know what it was?" he asked.

"No."

"A monkey's head."

"Oh no."

"And the head was still attached to a real live monkey! They had that sucker under the table all the time, then off with its skull. We were supposed to eat its brains while it was still alive!"

"You didn't, did you?" asked Terry, suddenly not very hungry.

"Well, I guess the guys could see I wasn't exactly up for the idea. But they had taken me out especially for a treat. I was stuck between a rock and a hard place. It would have been bad manners to refuse, but live monkey brains aren't my idea of fun either."

"So?"

"Well, as I said, they could see I wasn't up for it, so I invited them to go ahead and helped myself to more wine. The rest of the night is pretty fuzzy."

"You're a real gentleman, aren't you," said Mike. "Just as we're about to eat and all, you tell us that again."

"Sorry, guys," answered Andy. "You see, it affected me."

"Yeah, we can see that many things have affected you," joked Colin.

The evening continued, and as the alcohol settled deeper, the stories became longer. Andy, with his flashing eyes, wild hairy head, and animated expression, was the natural entertainer of the group. Terry thought it amazing how quickly Andy could forget something as serious as the fire and then ham it up as though nothing had happened. Mike cut a cooler, paternal image commensurate with his position, but the humor that shone from his eyes showed that he enjoyed Andy's company. The other fellows were younger and not as great characters but good company nevertheless. It was with difficulty that Terry bid them farewell and dragged himself away.

It was well after midnight when Terry tapped softly on the door of the hotel room.

"Tari, Tari," he called softly. After a while, he heard rustling from inside the room. There were footsteps, and the door opened to the length of the safety chain. His wife, bleary-eyed and still partly asleep, recognized him and released the safety catch. "How come you're late?" she asked.

"I got caught in a fire up at the camp." He kissed her gently and let himself in.

"Been drinking too," she stated.

"Yeah, we had a drink afterward." He looked at her affectionately. "You want to go back to sleep or hear the story?" he continued gently.

"Well, you'll tell me anyway, I guess, so why not now?"

Terry thus went through a brief description of the night's activities.

"So I wouldn't mind paying a visit to somewhere else while we're here," he said, looking over at her on the small bed where they lay.

"Uh-oh. Where?"

"The Melati oil field."

CHAPTER 8

They made their way northeast the following day to Pagaraya, another provincial town on the edge of the swampy eastern Sumatra flats. They arrived late in the afternoon, feeling dusty, dry, and fairly stiff. The minibus clattered to a halt, and Terry limped out after Lestari, again suffering circulation problems. It was a larger town than Taklin. Terry figured he could hire a car and driver to take him the sixty kilometers or so into Melati, which was fairly isolated in marshy terrain.

"These seats are not made for people with legs," he complained through his teeth as he hobbled away from the bus.

"Come on, hubby, whose idea was all this?"

They made their way through the crowded bus depot to a nearby hotel. The inevitable calls of "Hello, mister" and "*Belanda*" followed Terry wherever he went. There were not too many pale foreigners in this backwater province, so he was very noticeable. Nevertheless, they had a pleasant evening in the hotel which put Lestari in good spirits.

The next morning, they set about finding a car and driver, which was a more difficult task than both of them had anticipated. After tramping up and down the streets following directions, all they could get was an elderly man with an old army jeep; Terry couldn't decide which of the two, the jeep or the man, was the more ancient.

At midday, as agreed, the two antiques called at the hotel

to collect Terry and start the excursion. Lestari, rather than travel for hours through wetlands and jungle, chose to contact a relative in Pagaraya. Terry was amazed at the extent of Lestari's family. There seemed to be family relatives in every town of Indonesia.

"Take care," Lestari called as Terry climbed into the jeep.

"Will do, my love. See you later on tonight."

The ramshackle old vehicle bellowed to life and groaned into motion. Outside the town, it seemed to gather more spirit, and they were soon bumping along at a respectable rate. After an hour or so, they turned off the main road and onto a large dirt road, into the marshes toward the Melati field. Another hour saw them outside a swing gate barring the way. It was chained and heavily padlocked. There wasn't a soul about. Large warning signs on both sides declared *dilarang masuk*, "do not enter."

"Damn," swore Terry. He had expected a manned entrance he could bluff his way through. There was a guardhouse behind the fence, but it was empty and appeared not to have been used for a couple of months, judging by the dust and animal droppings. The fence itself stretched on either side into the marshy land a couple hundred meters; it was impossible for a vehicle to go farther. The lock and chains were too sturdy to break, and the gate had been welded, so it could not be unbolted. Beyond, the road stretched on through the wetlands, clumps of taller trees here and there marking higher ground. The sun was sinking lower, and in the distance, before the jungle started again, Terry thought he could make out a leveled wellsite and wellhead equipment.

"*Pak*, I want to run and look at that wellsite," he said to his elderly driver, pointing in the distance.

The crinkled face stared for a while where Terry pointed, obviously not relishing the idea.

"Be careful; many ghosts roam this land. I will not stay here past sunset."

"Okay," replied Terry, looking down the road beyond the gate. He thought he should be back by then. He had training shoes on his feet and was wearing shorts, so he took off his shirt, gathered it in his hand, climbed over the gate, and began jogging.

Eventually, sweating and tired, he arrived at what did turn out to be an old wellsite. A quick inspection of the wellhead, valves, and outlet pipe, about the same diameter as Terry's thumb, showed that it was not a strongly producing well by any means. It carried the identification "M-1" on a rusty plate wired to the side of the wellhead. Terry followed the outlet pipe back along to the service road. The jungle was quite near now, and Terry continued jogging along the road, thinking that he might find another wellsite not very far away.

His hunch proved correct, and another makeshift identification tag on the next wellhead declared "M-3." It was completed in the same way, with a thin pipe leading from it to join the other and carry on up the road. Closer inspection of the T-joint revealed a small leak, which dampened the earth not with oil but with water.

Terry stared at this for a while, reflective, until the raucous call of a jungle bird reminded him of the sinking sun. He had to return to the jeep before the old driver left without him. His body was stiff from his earlier jog and Terry had trouble coaxing his sore body into running again; he made slow progress. The sun sank lower and touched the horizon with a fluid kiss, illuminating the undersides of the heavy clouds in fiery reds and oranges. Terry was just under a kilometer from the gate as the last glimpse of sun winked out. He hoped that the old man would see him coming back.

After a painfully long time, he gasped up to the gate, leaning on it for support. The last of the fiery light was disappearing from the clouds, darkness was gathering, and the jeep had gone! His heart sank as he contemplated a night alone in the marshes. The ensuing panic evaporated his weariness, and he cast his eyes more intently along the gloomy track. He noticed with immense relief the stationary shape of the jeep at the limit of his vision in the twilight. He set off toward it, and as he drew closer, he saw that the hood was up. The old fellow had obviously meant to leave without him but had mechanical problems. As Terry came closer, he saw that the old man was checking the distributor and mumbling to nobody in particular; his movements were quite agitated.

"What's wrong, Pak?" asked Terry firmly as he walked around to the front.

The fellow jumped with fright and hit his head on the hood. He doubled over, holding his head painfully, and turned to face Terry, his eyes open wide in terror. Seeing Terry and not his worst fears, however, he relaxed a little.

"E...e...e...engine is dead."

The old man didn't know more than that, and it became apparent he did not have much mechanical knowledge at all. Terry replaced the distributor cap, put everything else back together, and tried to start the jeep. The engine turned but would not catch. He pulled off a spark plug lead and turned the motor; no spark. The old man told Terry he had this problem every now and then and fiddling with the distributor would normally fix it.

By this time, it was quite dark; only a slight gray was evident in the west. The old man produced a feeble penlight. His eyes frequently darted into the darkness, fearful of what might lie there. His fear was catching, and Terry also quickened his pace. The central spring-mounted contact in the distributor had been replaced with a piece of bent coat-hanger wire, and it was now not making contact. Terry cleaned and straightened it to a length where it would make the necessary electrical connection.

"That should do it," he said to the driver. Suddenly, the

weirdest cackle began from somewhere in the swampy wilderness. It was joined by another and then another until every direction echoed with the same maniacal laughter. It reached a frenzied crescendo and then began to fade. The old man froze in fear. The laughter was so close, Terry couldn't separate it from inside or outside his own head; his spine tingled, and goosebumps rose on his arm.

He jumped into the jeep and turned over the engine. It fired, died, and then caught again, emitting its own mournful bellow. The old man sparked to life, too, and climbed in beside Terry, gripping the door and slamming it shut. Terry found the lights and eased the old jeep into the beam. Far from the comfort of the lights of human habitation, the unfamiliar night had become menacing.

Sumatra, like the rest of the Indonesian islands, abounds in ghost tales though normally, Western people came and went without encountering anything unusual. Superstition and belief in spirits are firmly rooted in Indonesian culture, even with the influence of religion.

A few expatriates Terry had come across had experienced some extraordinary things. Terry remembered talking to a fellow from New Zealand, Steve, who had also worked on the Padang field development project and had a frightening experience with the supernatural. He had been sent to South Sumatra as a relief engineer, and, after taking part in a series of tests on a particular well, had to drive back to base by himself after midnight to pick up some extra equipment and rest before the next job scheduled on the well. He had been up for over twenty-four hours and was feeling pretty tired.

On the deserted main road back to his lodgings, after a period of time, he began driving automatically, and his mind retracted into his own thoughts. Some people drive for hours in this state and then can't recall any detail of the journey after they arrive. Slowly, however, he resurfaced from this condition, brought back by a feeling of some sort of presence behind him in the vehicle he was driving. He blinked his eyes and jolted fully awake, but the feeling that somebody was behind him remained. He became aware that the inside of the cab had become colder, yet he had not turned on the air-conditioner. The sensation of the faint scent of a woman also grew stronger. With his hands clenching the steering wheel tightly, he looked into the rearview mirror. In the dim light, he could see the shape of a woman with long hair. Her head turned toward the rear so he could not quite see her face.

Steve was very frightened and had an overpowering desire to turn fully around and look behind him. Another part of his mind was also aware, however, of an approaching right-angle corner before a bridge over a canal running parallel with the road. He had encountered this on his way out to the wellsite and had noted that it was a dangerous piece of road, particularly at night, when the bend was concealed by darkness. He felt that he was drawing near to this obstacle very quickly, but the compulsion to turn around toward the woman in the back was very strong.

His logical brain acted of its own accord, however, and his foot stomped on the brake. The vehicle skidded and swayed as the corner rapidly approached. In the glow of the headlights, he saw beyond the road a steep drop into an irrigation ditch off the main canal. Panic took hold of him, and he pressed harder on the brake, eventually bringing the vehicle to a slithering sideways halt a meter or so before the drop. He breathed out heavily with relief, and his shoulders relaxed into his seat. Then, remembering the ghostly apparition, he jerked to see what was behind. He found nothing. Gone were the chill and the scent. Hesitantly, he carried on, shaking with shock.

The next morning, Steve described his experience with others at the base and discovered that there was something strange about that particular place. Many vehicles had missed the corner and ended up upside down in the irrigation ditch at night, injuring or killing the occupants. The locals claimed it was haunted by a female spirit, whose house had been destroyed when the road went through.

"It was for real, man, no bullshit. The weirdest feeling I've ever had," Steve had said to Terry. Steve was convinced he'd seen something supernatural, and the intensity in his eyes convinced Terry that he hadn't made it up.

With these thoughts darting about his mind, Terry tried to urge as much haste out of the old jeep as possible. They bumped and lurched their way after the loom of the dim headlights. Strange and grotesque shadows were cast by bumps in the road and clumps of trees on the side. The way became more forested as they drew nearer the main road. Suddenly, the old man tensed and choked out an oath of some sort, his eyes wide in fear. Terry looked from him to the left-hand periphery of the headlight glow and also was charged with a shot of fright. He could just make out some phosphorescent motion about head high in the trees. Jamming one foot on the clutch and the other on the brake, he brought the vehicle to a stop just in front of this eerie sight.

It appeared to be a set of human legs swinging from the bough of a tree. No head, no body, just the legs, as though somebody invisible was sitting on the bough, dangling his legs downward and watching the traffic pass by. They were male legs, quite muscular, and glowed softly blue. Terry gaped in astonishment.

After a few moments, they started to fade from the thigh

down, until just the bare feet could be discerned. Then they too disappeared. Terry remained still for a while, wondering what he'd seen or what he imagined he'd seen. Then, from behind, he heard the same insane laughter they had heard earlier. It echoed in the distance above the sound of the idling jeep. The old man had slumped back in his seat and was mumbling to himself, probably a prayer of some sort. Terry snapped into action, forced the jeep into gear, and roared off.

They had not gone far, however, when the right-hand front tire went flat. Terry tried to drive on, but it was no use, as the tire was becoming shredded and would have to be changed. He stopped the jeep, though kept it idling, with the lights on. He looked at the old man, who pressed further into his seat.

"*Harimau!*" the old man croaked. "Tigers!" Then he began chanting again.

"Shit!" swore Terry. Either they would stay here all night, or he would need to get out to change the tire; both were not very attractive choices. He had become quite afraid and was extremely keen to get out of this weird night time chamber of horrors. Stepping out of the jeep and changing a tire in tiger country, though, wasn't an enthusing prospect either.

"Where's the jack and wrench?" he asked the old man, flicking on the light near the rearview mirror. Incredibly, it worked. The old man waved to their location and continued his solemn chanting. Terry grabbed what he wanted, sucked in deeply, quickly opened the door, stepped out, and went to work as fast as possible. There was enough light from the headlights to work, but, of course, the wheel nuts were stiff and needed lots of swearing and brute force to move. With his back to the dark as he worked on the wheel, his spine tingled. He succeeded in getting the wheel studs loose and then jacked the front up and wrestled the bad wheel off. He then went to the back for the spare, but it was bolted tightly to its support, and he didn't have the right-size spanner. Terry was sweating now and becoming flustered. He cursed the thing and climbed back inside the jeep.

"You have a screwdriver?" he asked the old man. The fellow pointed to the small front compartment. Terry opened it and pulled out a small screwdriver and then paused to calm his frayed nerves.

Pull yourself together, man, he chided himself.

When he was ready again, he went out and attacked the retaining bolt on the spare wheel, using the screwdriver as a chisel and the wheel wrench as a hammer. After too long, as far as Terry was concerned, it started turning and eventually could be loosened by hand. He yanked the wheel off, put it on the front, and started doing up the wheel nuts. As he was jacking down the vehicle, a staccato cry came from the jungle, and he heard something moving through the underbrush behind him. He grabbed the jack and spare wheel, threw them into the back, and jumped into the jeep as fast as he could, knocking his knee on the way in. He jerked the ancient vehicle into gear again and crunched off, leaving whatever was in the jungle to itself.

"What's wrong?" asked Lestari as she let him into the room. "You look like you've seen a ghost, and you're limping."

"I look that bad?" replied Terry. "Well, it's been a helluva night. I'm not too sure what I saw and what I imagined I saw, but it scared the hell out of me."

"Really, *sayang*, what happened?" she said soothingly. Terry was always humbled by her concern for him and marveled at her comforting powers. As they fell together on the bed, he began relating the night's experience.

After a long sleep, they rose late, packed up, and set off, first to wish farewell to Lestari's relatives, consistent with Indonesian good manners. This involved sitting down to some sweet tea and snacks, pleasant conversation, and lots of smiles. Terry was frustrated that they might miss the afternoon flight back to Jakarta but realized that the respect and goodwill they left behind was more important. As it turned out, one of the cousins offered to drive them to the bus station, so not much time was lost at all.

They caught a larger bus this time, though it was also short on leg room. Terry called these intercity buses ICBMs—intercontinental ballistic missiles—as they were driven as quickly and packed about as much punch. The drivers who pushed them around only seemed to know flat-out and stop. On the open road, they drove the buses as fast as they could go, their engines howling in protest. The drivers would pull out to pass slower traffic regardless of what was coming the other way. Motorbikes, minibuses, and passenger cars had to pull over to the side or would be crushed. With a flash of the lights to indicate "I ain't gonna give way," the driver would pull out into the other side of the road. Oncoming traffic had no choice but to pull over, as very little can stop an ICBM at full speed. It was all a question of size, and only a big Pratama tanker coming the other way would persuade the bus driver to slow down. Bus drivers knew the tanker driver would have the same view: "Might is right."

An ICBM meeting another ICBM posed an interesting problem, as in this case the "might" was the same. Normally there was a clear priority of who should maneuver first, but sometimes there was not, and it was decided by who had the most nerve and held on the longest. On other trips, Terry had seen two ICBMs on a collision course with each other—they simply swerved back to their own sides irrespective of what they were overtaking; those unfortunate vehicles were left with the muddy shoulder of the road to negotiate. On another occasion, Terry was taking a taxi with Lestari to Bandung, and an ICBM bearing its burden of humanity hooted and screamed past, sending oncoming traffic onto the edge of the road. "Bastard!" Terry had muttered.

Not more than five kilometers farther on, they came across the bus some twenty meters from the road in a paddy field on the right. The passengers were cautiously picking their way through the mud back to the road, some obviously shaken by the experience. Terry guessed that the bus driver had attempted to pass a large truck or tanker as another approached from the other direction; he must have lost his nerve and swung out into the rice field. Sometimes the drop from the road was not so gentle, however, and Terry had seen the upside-down remains of buses whose drivers had been as stupid but not so lucky. These accidents were very messy and caused huge loss of human life.

Terry hated riding ICBMs, but Lestari had used them occasionally and was not so worried. He figured the best thing was to sit in the middle of the bus and not look to the front. On the trip back to Pekanbaru, they found separate seats near the center. Terry sat next to a middle-aged fellow in typical formal Indonesian dress: sandals and dark trousers with a *batik* shirt and a black *peci*, symbolic of the Islamic faith.

The towns they passed were very tidy and seemed well-endowed with schools, hospitals, and even pavement. Most of the larger towns also boasted microwave antenna, and all had electricity. Terry remarked on this to his neighbor.

"Oh yes," replied the man. "There have been great changes here the last ten years. All children go to school, the infant mortality rate is now very low, and even family planning has been successful."

"That's good to see," replied Terry.

"Yes, you see, this is Bapak Siregar's home province, and he takes special care looking after it." Terry's ears pricked up at the name.

"He's a good guy, then?"

"Oh yes. Every time another school or hospital is built, he comes here personally to open it. He buys ambulances and even sends televisions to the hospitals. You see the irrigation canals here? This is also due to Pak Siregar. Now the farmers can make three crops of rice a year.

"Is it government money or his own?" Terry inquired.

"Oh, I don't know. As far as I know, it's government money, but Pak Siregar looks after it, making sure it doesn't get wasted. But we don't ask questions like that. My children can now go to school, they can be looked after if they are sick, and I can call my family in Java by telephone at my village post office. Why ask where the money comes from? That is rude in our culture."

"You're right, Pak," replied Terry. "I hope for continued success."

"I have no doubt that others will follow Pak Siregar's good example. Other provinces in Sumatra are now also developing, guided by his example here." He smiled a charming smile in typical Indonesian fashion, his tobacco-stained teeth flashing and eyes sparkling. "Perhaps before too long, Indonesia will be showing the way to the rest of the world."

Terry smiled back, indicating his approval.

CHAPTER 9

Some days after they arrived back in Jakarta, Terry sat outside on the porch of the Pantous' house in the quiet of the evening with Pop, Lestari's father. The throb of the countless individuals living all around was always present, though more subdued in the evening. There was a tiny garden, nothing more than a starfruit tree, really, to the side of the house. In front of the veranda where they sat, there was space for one car to park, and beyond that was the steel boundary fence and then the narrow lane that ran in front of the house and farther into the labyrinth of other houses. The housing complex was situated in Cempaka Putih, a middle-class area in Jakarta. It was very comfortable by Indonesian standards at the time but very cramped compared to Western standards.

The house itself was barely a hundred meters square but sheltered Mom and Pop, two sisters, two brothers, and the maid. It was very cozy right now, as Terry and Lestari were staying for a couple of nights. They had returned from Sumatra to their own house and found the letter from Exacom, signed by Ted Marsden, informing Terry that, after careful consideration, they decided his employment would finish at the end of the month. He had another month to pack up the house and move out. Another sheet of paper listed his termination entitlements. Terry rued that he had indeed been "terminated," such a dreadful word.

Mom and Pop had insisted that Lestari and Terry come

to Cempaka Putih and stay for a few days. Lestari confided to Terry that she thought Mom was worried that they would pack up too soon and leave for another job overseas. It was crowded but friendly in the family home, which is the Indonesian way. Both parents loved to see their daughter and son-in-law and to offer any support they could. So Terry and Lestari moved into one bedroom, Mom and Pop kept theirs, while the girls moved into the boys' bedroom and the boys into the living room. It was complicated but the accepted thing. Terry felt guilty displacing the boys, but Lestari and Mom wouldn't hear of it.

"We're used to living this close," they explained.

The evening was always pleasant in Cempaka Putih. It was as though every soul from the communal style of living sighed and relaxed at once. Over the inevitable cup of Indonesian coffee, Terry began telling Pop of their adventures in Sumatra.

"Yes," Pop said, after listening to Terry's account. "I've also seen strange things in Sumatra. While I was working on a rubber plantation, there was one ghost that people frequently saw. The locals say it came from a worker who was beaten to death by a Dutch overseer."

Terry settled down to listen. Before Pop had got very far, though, he noticed a military Land Cruiser moving slowly up the narrow lane. It was only using sidelights and was apparently looking for an address by the way it moved forward, stopped for a short time, and then moved on. The windows were very darkly tinted, so Terry couldn't see who was inside. The street was a cul-de-sac, and not too many vehicles passed this way. Pop stopped talking also to watch the approaching vehicle.

After a while, it pulled in front of the Pantou house and stopped. Two Indonesians emerged from the passenger side, checked the number on the gate, and looked in to see Pop and Terry watching from the porch. They were dressed in green khaki and sported military moustaches and short hair.

"*Selamat malam*," the more senior-looking one said.

"*Malam*," Terry and Pop replied.

"Are Terry and Lestari Miles residing in this residence?"

"Yes, that's right."

"We're from Banik, the government Internal Security Agency. Do you mind if we ask a few questions?"

"Not at all, come in," answered Pop, walking to the gate to let them in. They were led into the living room, and the traditional introductions were made.

"I am Sutri Wibowo, and my colleague is Prapto Sutrisno," the senior officer volunteered.

Mom offered tea and tried to hide her concern at being visited by officers of Banik. When all were seated and the formalities dispensed, Sutri began.

"No need to be concerned," he said. "We're just doing some routine checking following an incident at a cement factory near Pekanbaru yesterday. Your names were on the passenger list from Pekanbaru, so, in the interests of security, we'd like to ask you what you were doing in Sumatra." He looked at Terry and waited for an answer.

In the eighties, under the iron hand of President Suharto and his military force, there had been a certain amount of rebellion in the provinces against central rule. Often, this resentment was expressed through sabotage of infrastructure, as the locals saw projects such as cement factories conduits for wealth out of their province. Rebellion was particularly rife in the province of Aceh, which Suharto (and the Dutch before that) never did manage to squash into submission. An incident at a cement plant was not unusual. A visit by Banik officers, however, was.

"Well...er...we went up there on the spur of the moment, in fact," Terry stammered. "I...er...was told by my company,

Exacom, to take vacation unexpectedly before being transferred out of Indonesia. I have an old friend who works near Taklin for Asamera, and I wanted to see him before I left, so off we went."

"What is his name?"

"Andrew Herbert, a Canadian fellow. He had something I needed before I left Indonesia," Terry went on, embellishing the story slightly.

"Something that couldn't be sent to you after you left?" inquired Sutri.

"Maybe it could, but I couldn't trust Andy to send it," replied Terry, sweating a little. "He's that kind of guy."

"So tell me about this fellow and how we can get in touch with him. We need to cross-check, of course."

Surprised and relieved that he wasn't being pushed to reveal exactly what he had to get from Andy, Terry complied.

"We also went to Pagaraya," volunteered Lestari, "to see some of my mother's family." Mom nodded in agreement as Lestari outlined the complicated family tree. Terry was glad the heat had been taken off him, and he suddenly appreciated the family connections. After Lestari finished her elaborate description, Sutri nodded and asked, finally, "So you can prove that you went nowhere near the cement factory, then?"

"Of course we can. And whatever happened there?" asked Lestari. "Why would we be involved? We have no motive."

"So it seems," replied Sutri. "Well, we have to explore every avenue, you know. We still have many people to interview, so perhaps we should be going. Thanks very much for the tea and assistance."

The officers stood up, and the whole family bid them farewell before Pop, Lestari, and Terry saw them to their car.

Sutri and Prapto entered, and the vehicle reversed back down the lane. In the rear of the Land Cruiser, another military man asked a hunched-up figure, "Is that the one?"

"Yes, that's him," the figure replied. It was the old man who had driven Terry to Melati.

"That was pretty interesting," Terry said to the others back in the living room. "I wonder what all that was about. Did you see anything about a cement plant in the news, Pop?"

"No, though that doesn't mean that nothing happened," he replied.

"Our security service isn't that efficient, is it, Pop?" asked Lestari.

"Why not? Though I'm surprised that officers of such rank would attend a routine inquiry."

"How do you know what rank they were?" asked Terry.

"Oh, I was in the armed services too, and after a while, one gets a good feeling of what a soldier's rank is by his manner, how he speaks, and other things."

"Well, they seemed to be satisfied, maybe too easily," said Terry.

"That's just as well," replied Lestari, starting to smile.

"You can't tell a white lie very well, can you?"

"Oh, I don't know."

"Better leave storytelling in Indonesia to the Indonesians," said Lestari, smiling. "You don't know enough, my dear, to realize when you're saying something silly."

"You first mentioned Pagaraya, and he seemed very interested in that," he countered.

"Yes," murmured Pop, "he did." His eyes were glassy, and he had withdrawn to his own thoughts.

The bustle of life in Cempaka Putih was in full swing by the time Terry went out on the porch to talk to Pop the next morning. Vendors peddling fruit, cooking oil, satay, baso, meat, and numerous other items were already pacing the streets with their wares, making their characteristic calls.

Pop was clad in a sarong and white T-shirt, with a *peci* on his head and the paper on his lap. Sitting cross-legged in his chair wearing his reading glasses, he looked like a distinguished scholar.

"*Pagi*, Pop."

"*Pagi*."

"What do you know about General Siregar, Pop?" asked Terry as he settled down.

"Oh, this and that. Why do you ask?" Pop was always guarded when talking about public figures.

"Well, I don't know what to make of him; he's an enigma to me. On the one hand, he seems to be doing good for Indonesia; on the other hand, I've heard so many stories of the money he takes on the side for awarding contracts to foreign companies."

"Well, if he puts that money back into the country, it can't be too bad, can it?"

"But it's still corruption. It's still stealing, isn't it?"

"There are a lot of people who may benefit from this so-called stealing from a large foreign company, Terry, and remember, if it is as you say, those companies always have the choice to pay or not. They are willing to give whatever it takes."

"Then why isn't it done so that everybody knows where the money comes from and who it goes to?"

"Ah, Terry, you are so young and idealistic. Maybe the

general thinks that too much of the money will be frittered away in Indonesia's bureaucracy and not go to where it is needed."

"So it goes to the general, and how much of it is spent on himself and his supporters? Look at his lavish lifestyle."

"Yes, that's true, but you miss the Indonesian point of view here. I don't say that it is right, but certainly the people think that if a general is genuinely doing the country good, stimulating the economy, encouraging investment, improving communications, and so on, then they don't mind him keeping some for himself. This is how the village heads are supported and how the country was organized long before foreigners came to our shores. Why was Kirman allowed to go as far as he did with Pratama?" Pop was referring to the founding father of the state oil company. "The people thought that he was doing good for Indonesia, and despite the huge loss that he incurred by going too far on his ego trip, there are many things, like the refineries and steel plants, that are useful to Indonesia and are still here. Think of the jobs alone for ordinary Indonesians. That is the way people are here. Look at the support our own president has."

"But it's too open ended and subject to abuse."

"Maybe, but having lots of laws and doing things 'by the book,' as you say, doesn't prevent abuse either. Look at the way banks are attracted to third-world countries like vultures to dying prey. They swoop down and rape a country, legally. The way they courted Kirman himself was quite disgusting, like prostitutes around an open wallet. 'We'll give you help,' they said. 'Money is what you need.' Then the interest payments strike home, and all the money that should be spent stimulating the economy is siphoned out."

"But you have the choice also."

"Yes, very true. But unfortunately, Indonesians, who are not used to modern banking, are very susceptible to being duped.

As you know, in Islamic law, usury is a sin. But these foreign banks come in saying that they are going to help. Help themselves is all it amounts to."

Terry laughed. "You've really got it in for banks, then, Pop."

"Well, help is help. The Indonesian way of helping is, you help me, and I'll help you. That's the way the villagers have worked for centuries. We call it *gotong royong*, community spirit. This bank concept of hooking countries and then bleeding them is not the help we know."

"So, even if Siregar was helping himself a bit, you wouldn't object."

"As I've said, if he was doing good for his people, the people would think it his due to keep some for himself. And anyway, Terry, you just be careful what you say about Siregar and other leading figures. They do have a lot of support, and Indonesians are not as critical as the West when it comes to their leaders. You may get yourself into a lot of trouble."

"Sorry, sir, I take your point," Terry replied and lapsed into his own thoughts.

Pop was a wily old soul. He had been educated by the Dutch in Manado on Sulawesi and had good insight into the Western mind. From what Terry could learn from Lestari and Pop himself, he had lived a pretty interesting life.

He fled to Sumatra as a young man on board a *pinisi* (a sail-driven island trader), because the Dutch administration had forced him to interpret for them and be part of their, often brutal, administration. Their purpose was to extract as much out of Indonesia as they could. In Sumatra, he found work at a rubber plantation, where he again worked under the Dutch. Secretly, however, he had joined the Nationalist Movement and actually took part in sabotaging the plantation. The Dutch supervisors suspected the bright young clerk and set a trap for him. He was lucky to escape and took to the jungle, where he agitated the Dutch establishment in a guerrilla movement.

A price was put on his head, but before the Dutch could track him down, the Japanese arrived. Pop's group emerged from the jungle only to be rounded up by the Japanese "saviors" and forced to work in the oil refinery at Plaju, in South Sumatra. He witnessed a lot of atrocities carried out by the Japanese on his fellow workers as they forced their labor to work harder and harder to feed the imperial war machine.

Eventually, Pop and a few others managed to blow up some vital parts of the refinery and again escaped to the jungle. There they spent the rest of the war, harrying the Japanese when they could, but they were limited by their lack of arms and the small size of their group. Finally, the Japanese surrendered to the Allies, and when the renegades emerged from the jungle this time, they were given a hero's welcome. All became members of the Indonesian Army, which meant that the Dutch couldn't punish Pop when they returned to re-establish control over their colony. The days of the Dutch, however, did not last too long after the war, for Indonesia gained its independence in 1945 under the brilliant leadership of Sukarno. Pop then left the army, curiously enough, and married Lestari's mother. He set up a timber business with a partner and made a fortune.

When Lestari was young, they lived in a large house with running water and electricity provided by an outside generator, which was a luxury at the time. They also had one of the first new motorcars in Palembang. Always too trusting, Pop lost the lot when his partner double-crossed him and ran away with all their working capital. Pop was forced to sell the house and all the company assets that remained to cover their losses.

He then moved with the family to Jakarta and was asked

by an old acquaintance to help in a small engineering firm. Pop was mechanically adept and designed and built the first motorized people mover, the three-wheeled *bajaj*. He was cheated on once again when his friend sold the plans in order to recover gambling debts. The company that bought those plans probably made a fortune, based on the number of *bajaj* that have plied the streets of Jakarta over time.

A brother then found Pop a job in a Japanese refrigerator-assembling factory. Pop didn't like to work with the Japanese after what he'd seen them do to Indonesian people during the war, but he swallowed his pride in order to provide for the family. He started as the factory maintenance foreman and later became the manager for that department. His dislike for the Japanese emerged when he refused to go to Japan for a training program that would have given him another promotion. As a result, he attained no higher position.

When Pop took early retirement at the age of fifty-five, the factory directors were probably upset that they had lost a diligent worker but also relieved. As far as Terry could tell, his pension and contributions from the children, who were all working now, provided a comfortable life. Terry couldn't fathom all the complicated facets of the old gentleman's mind and, even from their last discussion, failed to discern Pop's real allegiance. He did sense that Pop had an inner strength despite his quiet exterior. Terry had discovered a similar strength in Lestari, which served to deepen his respect for her.

"Well, I guess I'd better start to look around for another job," said Terry after a long silence. "And I think that Singapore is a good place to start."

CHAPTER 10

Lestari managed to get airplane seats for both of them out to Singapore on the midday flight the following day. As was usual in that period of Indonesia's development, driving to the airport took longer than the flight. In those days they also had to negotiate the Halim International Airport, which was no more than a large open-air barn crammed with people.

During the hustle and bustle of departure formalities, they did not notice the young, tidily dressed man checking in behind them. He sat two seats behind them on the plane; he was dark and fit. He had short hair but did not have a moustache despite his military aura.

"So what's the plan when we get to Singapore?" asked Lestari when they were airborne.

"Well, I thought I would look up an old diver friend I used to see a fair bit of on projects I worked offshore."

"Diving? Surely finding a petroleum engineer like yourself would be better if you're going to find a job."

"Yes, when I start looking for a job. But there's something I want to do first."

"Like what?"

"Like find out what the hell is happening to the oil from Padang."

Lestari pursed her lips, and her dark eyes became troubled. "I hope you aren't thinking of something you will later regret."

Singapore hummed, driven by increasingly slick gears. Once a hot, humid, jungle-clad little island, it became a teeming center of trade, developing an affluence that made the rest of Asia envious. In the eighties, it already sported tall buildings, broad highways, and intertwined overpasses. Its airport was not only large but also efficient. Terry and Lestari were soon being whisked into the city in a large diesel taxi limousine. They passed along the east coast, with the large Marine Park recreation area on their left and high-rise apartment blocks on the right. At that time, most people were already living in such government-supported housing, squeezed from the sprawling villages (*kampung*) up into the new, clean towering apartment blocks prepared for them. The squalid, noisy communal village life still so prevalent in Jakarta had almost disappeared in Singapore. The development was spectacularly successful for health, safety, and land-optimization reasons, but Terry wondered whether the people had lost their soul after being displaced from their traditional dwellings. From what he'd seen and heard from Singaporeans on the rigs he visited, however, it seemed they were building a new identity and secretly were quite proud of what their country had achieved.

As Terry and Lestari passed closer to the sea, numerous cargo ships could be seen moored in the straits. Huge, inert tankers rose high out of the water with rounded bulbous fronts and abruptly terminated rears, the bridge and accommodation perched atop as though added as an afterthought.

The taxi climbed up over the East Coast Bridge, giving a spectacular view of the city center in the gathering evening. Then it swooped down and around to enter the urban traffic in central Singapore.

Terry and Lestari checked into one of the many modest three-star hotels downtown.

"We're unemployed now," joked Terry. "So we'd better lay low for a while."

"Well, it's comfortable enough," commented Lestari. "What are we going to do now?"

"Find the Mine of Information, Singapore-style," replied Terry. "The Jockey Pub."

"You know all those types of places," she said in disgust.

"Does that mean you're coming?"

"Terry, don't be so rough."

"Sorry, *sayang*," he said in a softer voice. "Well?"

"Well what?"

"Well, are you coming?"

"I suppose there's going to be sweeties there?" Lestari asked, referring to the usual working girls who made themselves available to oil patch men for the night.

"I suppose you're right."

"Humph!"

"What language is 'humph,' and does it mean you're coming or not?"

Lestari said nothing.

"I gather from your silence," continued Terry, "that this is your usual protest against bars and such places and that I'm to suffer with the silent treatment for as long as you feel I need to get the point." He then changed tack, smiled gently, and went to give his wife a hug. "I'm sorry, my love. I guess I'm a little tired and distracted. It's still early, and I'm sure you'd like to go somewhere nice to eat first, eh? How about it, gorgeous? One romantic meal for two in Singapore?" He squeezed her tightly.

"Not happy," she stated but was obviously placated by the option. "You're impossible."

"Okay, let's shower and get out of here. How long do you need to get ready? An hour or two?" he joked, knowing that he was treading on dangerous ground.

"A long time…" Terry could see he'd won her over.

They had a pleasant meal in one of the better restaurants that lined Orchard Road, preferring quiet European-style to hectic, though tasty, Chinese. The shops were still open, and Lestari had time to browse, so they arrived at the Jockey Pub in good spirits. It was rather small and set in the style of an English pub, with horse racing as its theme. Pictures of horse races and horses lined the walls, along with ribbons, polished leather bridles, and all sorts of other racing paraphernalia. The draught beer taps were also fashioned as horses' heads, and the wooden furnishings gave an Old English atmosphere. It was a comfortable place for the Western expatriates and served as a convenient meeting place.

Lestari and Terry walked in through the heavy wooden saloon doors, and inevitably, many people looked around. The "sweeties" who had not yet found partners zoomed in on Lestari, instantly raising her hackles and damping her good spirits. The available girls, for their part, quickly sensed that the new man wasn't available and tried to conceal their disappointment by feigning boredom.

"C'mon, let's get a drink," urged Terry, and he led Lestari to the bar and the few remaining empty stools. "One beer and an orange juice, please."

As he waited, he gazed around the room, trying to find a familiar face. Before too long, he recognized someone from the rigs he had worked on. "There's a guy I know," he said to Lestari. "Damn, what's his name, though? I remember a string of faces and characters, but I'm hopeless at putting names to them all."

"What does he do?" asked Lestari.

"He's a mud man."

"A what?"

"A mud man."

"Doesn't sound too flattering."

"A mud doctor. He makes up the mud that is pumped down around the drill bit while the well is being drilled."

"Well, I'm glad you're not a mud man, dear. I wouldn't like to tell my friends that my husband made mud."

"It's an important job. In fact, the wrong chemicals in the mud can lead to disaster. These guys sit on rigs a long time, though. His size is due to the good rig food they eat. Joe—that's his name! There's so many Daves, Bobs, Jims, and Joes, it's confusing. Let's go over there and start finding out a few things."

"What are you after in particular?"

"An Aussie diver who used to be on the Seagull rig we used in Padang. This intrigue would be right up his alley."

As they took their drinks and walked around the bar, they did not notice the single *pribumi* (native Malay) enter. He was dark, athletic, and dressed in casual tennis shirt, jeans, and sneakers. The sweeties all tried to give him their best eye, immediately attracted by his singleness. He had a rather aloof manner, however, and ignored all the stares. He walked up to one of the stools recently vacated by Terry and Lestari and ordered a whiskey on the rocks.

"It's Joe, isn't it?" inquired Terry when he approached the large man, who had sideburns so long, they almost made a beard.

"Yeah, that's right. Joe Sparks," the man replied, turning to greet Terry. He was dressed in fairly typical oil-patch apparel, which meant jeans, leather boots, a large belt buckle, and a peaked cap, but instead of the standard checked collared shirt, he sported a black T-shirt that only just managed the job of covering his belly.

"Let's see, you're with Exacom, right?"

"I guess I'm not anymore. I'm Terry, and this is my wife, Lestari."

"Lucky guy. I've been looking all over for a gal like that."

Lestari froze at the cursory greeting he gave her and the chauvinistic overtones.

"We've just arrived in Singapore, and I'm trying to track down Jeff Palfrey. Do you know him? He's an Aussie diver."

"Let's see now...he's not the guy who is working in Singapore now, at some dive-tour place?"

"Could be. He always said it was what he wanted to get himself set up in."

"What did he look like?"

"Red hair and freckles but a solid guy, looked like he pumped weights."

"Yeah, that's the one. Don't see him around too much now. I guess he's busy with tours and stuff."

"Where's he located? Do you know?"

"No, but the bar manager might. Hey, Othman!" he called to the bar manager near the cash register. "C'mon here, we need you." The smiling Singaporean obliged, amply experienced with rough oilfield people who ordered him around like arrogant colonists.

"Y'know an Aussie diver—what's his name?"

"Jeff Palfrey," answered Terry.

"Ah yes, Mr. Jeff," responded Othman, after reflecting for a little while. "We don't see him much now, but he left some cards behind the bar. He make his own business at diving and ask me to promote a little bit."

"Could I have one, then?" asked Terry. "I'm an old friend of his."

"Okay, no problem." Othman went off to rummage through

some drawers.

"Well, that's good news. I reckon that deserves a drink. Want another one?" Terry inquired.

"Yes, I'm about ready for another."

Othman returned with a card.

"Two more beers, please," Terry said. He felt Lestari nudging his arm.

"Yes, mister, this is Mr. Jeff's card."

"Thanks." Terry read, "'Singapore Tropical Dive Tours, Jeff Palfrey, Dive Master–Tour Manager.' Sounds pretty good," he said, showing it to Joe.

"Yeah, I guess he's with all them rich tourists now. He was a good hand."

Terry kept Joe chatting through the next beer. Small talk, rig talk, male talk. He sensed Lestari's growing impatience.

When he finished his beer, he put the empty glass on the bar and tried to finish the conversation politely.

"Well, Joe, good to see you again. We'd better be pushing off now. Take care."

"Okay, guys, look after yourself too."

They paid their bill and filed out. The place had become quite full, with standing room only. The sweeties all appeared to be busy, chatting with men, turning on their charms.

In the arcade outside, Lestari said, "Wait a minute, Terry; let's stop behind here for a while." She steered him behind a column before the down escalator.

"What's going on?" asked Terry.

"Shh," Lestari whispered. "Didn't you notice the Indonesian policeman sitting by himself who came in after us?"

"Nope. Anyway, how do you know he's Indonesian? Or a policeman?"

"I can tell. Anyway, he didn't seem to fit in that place; he wasn't very comfortable and kept looking at us."

"Maybe he wanted to pick you up."

"Terry! I want to see if he follows us out."

They waited a couple of minutes, but the fellow didn't appear.

"Hmm, interesting. Doesn't look like he's coming," said Terry. "Let's go."

"Yes," said Lestari reluctantly. "Oh, well. He gave me the creeps, anyway."

They moved out of the arcade and into the street.

"Well, do you want to go somewhere?" asked Terry. "A disco, maybe?"

"Not really. I'm a bit tired, and that guy made me nervous."

"Okay, let's get a taxi back."

As they climbed into a taxi at a nearby taxi stand, another dark, wiry fellow broke out of the crowd and pushed his way into another cab.

Meanwhile, in the Jockey Pub, the first watcher was talking earnestly to Othman, the bar manager. They were leaning over the bar looking at another "Singapore Tropical Dive Tours" card, held by the other man.

"See that?" urged Lestari. She turned to face the rear.

"What now?" asked Terry.

"I saw a guy jump into that taxi, and it's following us."

"Everybody seems to be following us," teased Terry.

"Seriously, Terry, watch him."

Terry gave some new instructions to their taxi driver, an old, wrinkled and balding Chinese man. The taxi Lestari pointed out did seem to follow.

"Yeah, looks like you're right," said Terry after a couple of turns. "What do you want to do?"

"I don't like it!"

"Okay, but whoever it is, has been following us for some time and knows where we are staying. If we lose them now, they'll pick us up there."

"Well, I don't like being followed like this."

"Okay." Terry leaned forward to the driver. "It looks like somebody is following us that we don't want. Can you lose them?"

The old man's thin mouth opened, revealing discolored teeth as he chuckled. "Hundred dollars," he said. "Singapore money. Yes?"

"A hundred dollars!" exclaimed Terry. Then he thought about it. "Okay, a hundred dollars if you lose them, nothing if you don't."

"I lose them." The old man chuckled. He swerved suddenly to the left down a small street and then accelerated quickly. Terry and Lestari were flung across the back seat. The vehicle then went down a slight decline, horn blaring, headlights flashing. The few people left in the street at that time of night jumped for their lives. A sharp left down another lane and then shortly another left, squealing tires, raucous engine protesting over the unaccustomed work it was being asked to do. This brought them back to the major one-way road they started from.

The driver pushed his way in, still chuckling and smiling, and worked his way right, checking the small road they exited from in the mirror. Terry also looked back and saw the lights of the taxi they were trying to lose emerge a hundred meters or so behind. The old driver noted this and smiled some more, now that he had assessed the skills of who he was trying to lose.

Sharp right this time, no warning, another small side street, severe acceleration, fifty meters or so and then a squealing, slithering stop and left. On the gas, the horn, a couple of streets and then right, and so on. Late-night trishaws and dogs leaped to the side as the blaring, crazy taxi rushed by. Before too many turns, though, the old man eased his pace and went longer between turns, still keeping to the back alleys that he obviously knew as well as his own home. They passed through one small winding street and then under a railway bridge before Terry was satisfied they had lost their tail.

"Okay, let's go back to the hotel, get our stuff, and disappear again," said Terry.

"This is getting too much."

"It's this or being watched all the time."

"Why are we being watched?"

"Beats me. Maybe somebody is afraid we're going to be naughty," replied Terry. "Anyway, let's melt away for a while."

"Okay," Lestari replied unenthusiastically.

Terry turned to the driver.

"Okay, you've got a hundred dollars extra, now would you like some more?"

"Yes, mister, thank you; no problem, mister!"

Terry told him the hotel where they were staying and asked if there was a back way in.

"Yes, mister. Very good for you. Rear door on back street. I park there, you bring baggage, I waiting."

When they tried the back door, however, they found it locked at that time of night.

"Okay, so we go in the front," said Terry to the driver. "You drop us off as normal, then come around here. Here's what I owe you, and there's more if we get out of here without anybody following."

They walked into the foyer and then took the key to their room. Two *pribumi* (native Malays) were sitting in the coffee shop opposite and followed their movements.

Terry and Lestari packed their belongings quickly and took them to the first floor, down the fire exit to the ground, and along a corridor, out of view of the foyer, to the rear exit, where they let themselves out. Terry packed the gear into the taxi while Lestari stood inside the rear exit. She let him back in, so he could pay the bill. It was tempting not to pay, but they weren't criminals yet, and they could be traced through the credit-card imprint. He went to the front desk and apologized to the cashier, saying that they had found some friends in Singapore who invited them to stay immediately.

"So could we pay the bill and check out?"

"And your baggage, sir?"

"We'll be ready in ten minutes."

Fortunately, it wasn't a multi-star hotel with minibar billing complications.

When this was done, Terry walked to the elevator and took it to the first floor, where he let himself out of the hotel again, the same way the baggage went.

The Malays had in the meantime moved to the front desk and were asking questions of the cashier who had just checked Terry out. They then moved quickly to the car park at the front of the hotel. A car sprang to life, and they ran toward it.

The old man had his taxi warmed up as Terry clambered in.

"Let's go to a hotel where you can check in any time you like, and nobody asks questions. Understand?"

"Yes, mister, understand." He pulled out at a normal pace as a car screeched into the lane behind them, its lights illuminating them in the narrow back street.

"Uh-oh!" said Lestari.

"A hundred dollars," called Terry.

The taxi roared and leaped forward into the night.

The tail was a little more difficult to shake off this time. What their followers lacked in local knowledge, they made up for in horsepower and aggression. They became engulfed in a weird night world of flashing lights, wild motion, and a cacophony of whining engines and screeching tires. They briefly found themselves back on a main road and jumped a red light (Lestari ducked her head in panic as the traffic approached from opposite directions). The pursuers, close at this stage, also escaped through. However, a waiting police car spotted the pair and bolted after them, siren wailing, lights flashing.

"Oh shit!" said Terry. "Now we've got trouble." The police in Singapore at that time used small, though high-powered, BMWs and were trained for high-speed chases. The old Chinaman driver nodded but didn't show any sign of nervousness. He stomped on the brake and then turned sharp left. Their followers also turned sharply behind, and the police soon after, gaining quickly.

The side street was narrow but straight. The more powerful cars drew up quickly to the laboring taxi. It wasn't long before they were looking for a place to overtake, almost bumper-to-bumper. Lestari's face was stark with fright in the blinding headlight glare. The road opened up and swept to the right. The second car swung over for the gap on the right and began to overtake.

The taxi, however, veered suddenly left. Terry raised his arm, anticipating a crash, but they entered a well-hidden narrow lane that bore left off the other road. The overtaking car braked hard and attempted to lunge left also, but it was too late. The car slid sideways and smashed its rear into a concrete barrier on the right of the small lane. It came to a halt straddled across the lane. The police car was following too closely (excitement had got the better of caution) and couldn't stop in time. It slammed into the stationary vehicle, making a dull thud as its expensive German bodywork bent.

Lestari sighed deeply. Her knuckles were sore from tightly gripping the door handle on one side and Terry's arm on the other. Terry also breathed with relief. He rubbed the arm that was sore from Lestari's vicelike grip. The old taxi driver chuckled his dry cackle and continued on sedately.

"Bastard planned that all the way," whispered Terry tightly. "Wonder how many irate mistresses he's thrown off back there!"

"This is getting too much," repeated Lestari, her voice wavering.

"Tell me about it."

"What are we going to do?"

"Well, we're in it now, baby, whatever it is. Let's get some rest and think it over. Very good, sir," said Terry to the taxi driver in his everyday business voice. "Now, can you take us to that quiet hotel where people don't ask questions?"

The old taxi driver clicked his tongue, nodded, and started moving through the streets again with renewed purpose.

The decrepit, partially illuminated sign declared "Blue Sky Hotel." It hung dejectedly above the portal of a dilapidated building squeezed between darkened shopfronts on a side street somewhere in Singapore.

Terry paid the taxi driver his princely sum. The old man accepted it with a half-grin and pushed a card into Terry's hand, as if to say, "Next time you want the same service, call me." With all the restrictions and laws forcing Singaporeans to be model citizens at that time, there wasn't much adventure to be had on the island, and the taxi driver obviously relished any excitement he could get.

They went up through the doors to the small foyer, where a large middle-aged lady sat behind a desk reading a Chinese magazine. She looked at the pair from behind thick glasses, carefully evaluating what she saw.

"A room for two, please," said Terry. The woman eyed Lestari up and down, making her feel very nervous.

"For how long? Special rate for one hour—twenty dollars, plus cleaning five dollars."

"Oh no, we want for longer than that. We want to rest until midday at least."

The lady turned to Lestari and asked again in rough Malay, obviously thinking she was escorting the white tourist.

"I'm sorry, I don't understand," replied Lestari furiously in English. "I am from Indonesia, and we're visiting Singapore."

The old lady grunted and pushed a form and a pen at Terry, and, mumbling under her breath, went to a cabinet and withdrew a key. Terry signed some fake names and passport numbers and reached for the key.

"Fifty dollar," said the woman before handing him the key.

"Pay now?" asked Terry.

"No pay, no room," replied the woman.

He handed over the money and took the key.

Their room was on the second floor, overlooking the street. An old cage elevator took them there, clanking and jerking in a way that did not inspire confidence. Terry opened the door of their room and turned on the light.

"Jeez!" he exclaimed. "Take a look at this!" The room was decorated mostly with mirrors, erotic-looking ornaments, and posters.

"Ugh!" declared Lestari. "Disgusting place."

120

"No doubt what trade this joint is into," said Terry. "Anyway, let's catch some sleep."

"This is stupid. How much more stupid is it going to get?" she said, coming over to him for some comfort.

"I don't know, honey. I hope not much more." He held her close. The chase, the excitement, and the weird surroundings stimulated some animal passion, however, which they consummated before finally lying down to rest.

Even then, rest was not easy, due to the heavy patronage of the hotel. Cars came and went, voices rose and fell, giggles came from along the corridor, the weary elevator clanked, thuds and pleasure screams came from adjacent rooms. At one time there came a knock on the door. Terry drowsily went to open it and found a scantily clad girl outside, made up and ready for business.

"Mister like a nice massage from Rosy?" she cooed. Terry closed the door without replying.

"I'll never stay in a place like this again," Lestari told him when he returned to bed.

At dawn, though, the activity subsided, and the pair drifted into slumber until the daytime street noises outside brought them to.

A telephone rang in the quiet hall of a magnificent large mansion. A servant in an immaculate black and white uniform answered it. After a short while, he picked up the remote receiver and went outside into the early-morning sunlight, where a powerful older Asian man was toweling himself off after a morning swim. He had metal-gray hair and a large moustache and was still in good physical shape despite carrying some extra weight. The man grumbled to the manservant.

"I thought I didn't receive calls before six."

"It's from Omar in Singapore," replied the servant. "He says it's very urgent."

The impressive master grabbed the receiver and demanded gruffly, "What is it?"

He then listened attentively while stroking his moustache. After a short time, his mouth worked, and his face wrinkled as though he was not enjoying the news.

"You did what?" he asked. "How the hell could you do that?" He slapped his forehead with an open palm. "I can't believe this incompetence. Who was driving? I'll have his neck!" The speaker was obviously quite ashamed and apologetic to his chief. "What was that? Oh good, one small bit of intelligent work." He listened some more, his rage subsiding. "Okay, well, when they show up, just watch them and keep me informed, have you got that? I want them watched, not run down!" He clicked the receiver off, threw it onto a nearby table, and jumped into the swimming pool again to cool off.

CHAPTER 11

Lestari was particularly relieved to depart from the Blue Sky and its nocturnal life. By the time they finally checked out, it was closing on midday. Both were still drowsy as they took a taxi to Singapore Tropical Dive Tours. This turned out to be located in a two-story commercial building constructed to service the North Shore Marina. There was also a marine chandlery business, a dive retail shop, a café, and a tourist information kiosk in the same building. They entered the front office on the lower floor, which was adorned with photos of dive trips, brochures advertising dive tours, and a variety of diving equipment.

"Is Jeff Palfrey here?" Terry asked the Malay girl at the front counter. Her lithe form and sun-darkened skin indicated that she enjoyed an outdoor life.

"Oh, Mr. Jeff? He is at the marina," answered the girl, passing an intense gaze over Lestari.

"Can we see him, please? We're friends from overseas."

"Well, okay," she said uncertainly. "He is very busy." Nevertheless, pointing to a schematic diagram under the glass of the counter, she gave directions to the marina and showed at which berth they would find Jeff.

"The boat is called *Sea Speed*. Mister Jeff is there."

They thanked her and left for the short walk through the marina to the boat.

"Anybody home on *Sea Speed*?" Terry shouted at the

large motor launch when they located it. The *Sea Speed* looked appropriately named; she was sleek and appeared very fast. She also had a large working area aft and easy access from the stern for diving.

A blond mop of hair popped up from a front hatch. A freckled face looked at the pair on the jetty through blue eyes and smiled as he recognized Terry.

"Terry, mate," he said, beaming. "How yer going? Wotcha doin' here?" His Australian accent was very obvious.

"We're all right. This is my wife, Lestari."

"G'day," Jeff said to Lestari, his smile lines crinkling further. "Some blokes have all the luck, ay?"

Lestari couldn't help but be disarmed by this friendly fellow and smiled back. He actually met her eyes and did not shrug her off as merely an accomplice to Terry, as so many other oilfield men had the habit of doing.

"What about yourself?" asked Terry.

"Up to me cobblers in problems, mate," Jeff replied. "I've just 'ad a Chinese group cancel on me. We was 'sposed to leave this mornin' for a week up the east coast. I keep the deposit, but it doesn't pay all the bills. I'm just gearing up for day trips to fill in. And what are you doin' in these fine parts?"

"We've come to see you, of course," replied Terry, laughing. "But we've also got a problem. I reckon you'll be interested in hearing about it."

"Dunno about that, sport. I've got a few beauties of me own in this outfit. What's the score?"

"Well, we seem to be wrapped up in some sort of intrigue we can't understand. It's got something to do with the Padang oil field, and we're being followed all the time."

"Oh yeah?" replied Jeff, his interest rising. "You'd better come aboard. We'll yarn over a cuppa." He pulled his sun-bronzed, muscular body from the hatch and came over to help them aboard.

The watchers from the waterfront car park observed the three disappear into the vessel.

"Shall we get closer?" asked one, lowering his binoculars.

"No point," said the other. "Where can they go? You've got the name of the boat?"

"Yes, *Sea Speed.*"

"Okay, well, we had better not make the boss more upset. We just have to watch."

Jeff listened intently as Terry elaborated on what had happened, from his experience in the Padang field and their visit to Sumatra to their car chases through Singapore. Jeff's growing interest was evident; he was a boy at heart and loved a good adventure. Terry embellished the story appropriately.

"Something screwy's goin' on for sure," mused Jeff as Terry finished.

"The problem is what to do now," said Terry. "I think that some big scam is going on with the Padang field. Someone knows I know something about it but not how much I know. We really want to stop being hassled, but this is big bucks, and I can't see how to escape."

"Unless you go to the press and make it all public knowledge."

Terry was hoping Jeff would be led to that conclusion.

"I like that idea, but I haven't got any hard evidence for what's happening. All the data is in my head. I don't have an official report, or, in fact, anything except my personal account and suspicions."

"Well, let's get some!" volunteered Jeff.

"How?" asked Terry.

"The boat needs a run. Let's zip across the Malacca Straits and find some!"

This was more than Terry had hoped for.

"Are you sure?"

"No worries, mate!" said Jeff. "We're all ready to go, and nothing much interesting has been happening around here, anyway. The boss is away, so let's go!"

"When?"

"Tonight!"

"Can we do it in a night?"

"You bet, man! We're at the end of a perfect weather window, and this bugger can haul arse. I know the area well enough; I've been there from time to time."

"What about clearance to get across into Indonesian waters and all that business?"

Jeff smiled. "Don't worry about that, mate. There's more boats crossing that Strait at night smuggling than you could point a stick at. And they ain't slow old fishing boats."

Terry had caught Jeff's natural enthusiasm and was smiling along with him. Lestari, on the other hand, was more unsettled. This was a completely different world for her, and she didn't particularly like it.

"What if we're still being watched?" asked Terry.

"Good point. But I know how we can sort that one out."

In the late afternoon, the watchers saw the three re-emerge

from the launch and climb onto the jetty. They stopped to talk for a while, and then there was handshaking and back-slapping as though farewells were being bid. The target couple then departed, waving as they went. The blond man returned to the launch and, after going below for a short time, reappeared with some hand tools and started working on a fitting on the antenna mast.

Following the two targets was an easy task, as their backpacks made them fairly conspicuous. The watchers left their car and followed. Terry and Lestari seemed to be following directions from a piece of paper that Terry frequently pulled out of his top pocket and referred to.

They moved through the waterfront streets, which were crowded with harbor activity and colorful people: sailors, agents, tourists, and businessmen. After a while, they stopped outside one of the hotel bars that were common in the area. Lestari appeared surprised that he stopped and looked at her partner inquiringly.

Some discussion followed, with Lestari pointing frequently at her wristwatch. One of the Indonesians found a shop window to gaze into while casually observing the two. The other had become the 'watchers' watcher and was a farther distance behind. Terry seemed to win Lestari over, and she gave a shrug of resignation. The two then went inside the bar. The first watcher slowly walked toward the entrance, wondering whether he should go in. From the actions of Terry and Lestari, he surmised that it was an unplanned stop. After waiting for some minutes, he checked that his accomplice was close enough and indicated that he would go in while the other fellow waited.

He entered the main swinging doors into a small hallway. There was an entrance to a coffee shop on the right and another entrance to a bar on the left. A small reception desk was in the middle in front of the stairs that led up to the guest rooms on the upper floors.

First, he tried the coffee shop; they weren't there. Then, trying to look as casual as possible, he tried the bar. They weren't there either.

He went back to the reception desk and asked the bored looking Chinese girl, "Did you see two people come in here not very long ago? One was a European man, the other an Asian lady, both wearing backpacks."

"Sorry, sir," she replied in poor English. "I just start. I not see anybody. Maybe the girl before me see."

"Where is she?"

"She go already."

"But they were here two minutes ago."

"Yes, and I start just one minutes ago."

"Well, your friend can't have gone far. She must still be here."

"She go quickly. She say mother-in-law very angry, must go home fast."

The watcher was frustrated but thought further discussion was worthless. He asked the waiter in the coffee shop and then the barman in the bar.

"Sorry, sir, nobody like that came in here. I would notice them for sure," replied the barman.

"Well, is there a back entrance to this place?"

"Well, yes," replied the barman, becoming suspicious.

"Can you show me?"

The barman quickly ascertained that the visitor was police or military by his tone of voice and manner of asking questions. His use of English showed that he was not from Singapore either. He judged that it was better to comply, nevertheless.

"Okay, just a minute." He rang an internal buzzer, and shortly a colleague appeared. He gave the barman a subtle, knowing wink and led the visitor back to the hallway, past the receptionist, and to a passage behind the stairs.

"Here you are, sir," the guide said as he opened the rear door at the end of the passage.

The watcher looked out on a long narrow alley, to the left, and the right. Rubbish was piled near the back entrance of every building. He couldn't see the targets on either side, and it looked like some distance from the door before anyone could turn off. He swore under his breath.

"Okay, thank you. I've lost somebody, that's all."

"Well, I hope you find them, sir."

The first watcher walked quickly back to his friend outside. After a brief discussion, they parted and walked briskly in opposite ways around the block, meeting in the rear alley. This and further inquiries, however, didn't provide them with any success.

"In the name of Allah! Where'd they go?"

"Maybe back to the marina."

They ran to get a taxi and then urged the driver back to the marina at full speed. From the car park, they peered out into the pens of boats. The marina lights were flickering on in the gathering darkness, and the *Sea Speed* was gone.

Some distance away, out of the sight of the watchers, its sleek dark shape slowly glided up to a general-purpose pier, where Terry and Lestari were waiting.

When they had entered the hotel earlier, they had turned directly left into the main bar and went straight to the barman. The bar itself was clean but well used, featuring fading wood paneling and nautical decorations. A few groups of men were engrossed in their own conversations and drinks. Terry pushed a card Jeff had given him toward the barman and said, "We need to use the little room."

"Ah, okay," replied the barman after a small hesitation. "Come this way," he said, beckoning. He also reached for the nearby intercom and said a few words to the receptionist outside in a local dialect. He led them through a door by the side of the bar and through a dingy and dimly lit hall at the rear of the building. They passed a number of curtained partitions before arriving at a more substantial-looking door at the far end. Their guide operated a mechanism that withdrew all the bolts and opened the door. On the other side was a two-bay garage containing a taxi and driver, who was already starting the vehicle.

"You get in, and the driver take you where you want," said the barman.

"Who fixes this up?" inquired Terry.

"Part of the service," said the man with a half-smile.

Terry and Lestari clambered into the back seat, the garage door slid open, and they drove out into the narrow alley. The door shut silently behind.

"Well, that's pretty neat," remarked Lestari. "Who would normally use such a thing?"

"Husbands wanting to slip off and see their mistresses or girlfriends, I guess," replied Terry. "Or maybe boyfriends wanting to elude the angry husbands of their girlfriends."

"Ugh, there seems to be more time and effort spent on having illicit relationships than on developing married relationships."

"You're right there, my love. It seems to be a feature of Asia."

She pinched him firmly in disgust.

CHAPTER 12

Sea Speed quietly glided to the rendezvous point. Terry and Lestari quickly jumped down from the pier over the bow. A mechanical thunk signified that reverse had been engaged, and the burbling engine note rose slightly as the vessel moved back. The pair clambered around one side, dumped their gear on the back deck, and climbed up to the darkened flybridge, where Jeff was at the controls.

"G'day," said Jeff, his head and hands not moving from their purpose. "Glad you made it. Hang on a minute while I get us out of here." He swung the bow out to sea, selected forward gear, and applied some throttle. The engine noise became a powerful hum, and the boat darted forward, raising a hissing bow wave.

"How do you get to know such places?" asked Terry after a while, when the lights upon Singapore harbor were passing by regularly.

"You mean the bar back there?" asked Jeff. Terry nodded. "Oh, I did a favor for the guy who owns it. I found something he'd dropped into the sea. Anyway, he lets me use disappearing privileges whenever I like. It comes in handy from time to time with over-possessive girlfriends." He turned and smiled boyishly at Lestari.

"I can imagine," said Terry. "So, what's the scoop now, then?"

"Well, mate, let's get out of here without attracting too

much attention. Then we motor up the Straits and duck over to Padang Island when the coast is clear. Why don't you go below and find a cabin to dump your gear into? Help yourself to some grub in the galley and get a billy on the boil for a cuppa. You can get some shut-eye too, if you like."

"Roger, dodger," replied Terry. "C'mon, Tari, let's get organized."

After stowing their gear in a vacant cabin, Terry managed to get a kettle boiling on the gimbaled gas stove. A chart of the Malacca Straits had been laid out on the chart table, and Terry began studying it.

"Have you forgotten about me?" interrupted Lestari. He looked up at his pretty but tired-looking wife, obviously in need of some attention.

"Of course not, *sayang*," he said, smiling, rising to embrace her. "Why don't you get some sleep?"

"If I can. I'm not used to the movement of boats. Anyway, I need a hug." They held each other until the shrill whistle of the boiling kettle interrupted.

"I'd better get the captain a cuppa," said Terry. "Do you want anything?"

"Not really." Lestari shrugged. "I think I'll go and lie down." He led her into the cabin and made sure she was settled before getting back to making a cup of tea. The motion of their passage became rougher, and the vessel's speed increased, so Terry had to take more care not to spill anything.

"I hope your tea is how you like it, sir," joked Terry as he climbed up to the flybridge with a steaming cup.

"You beauty, mate," rejoined Jeff, taking it from him and

sipping. "Yeh, that's pretty bloody all right. Where's the missus?"

"Down below, trying to sleep. How're we going?"

"Aw, it's a bit rougher than I would have liked. I can't open her right up. Maybe when we get around the tip of Malaysia, it will be smoother. But we'll get there."

"How do you drive this thing, anyway?" asked Terry.

"Yeh, I'd better show you. You never know what might happen. Jeez, it's gonna be a long night."

The silhouette of *Sea Speed* cut through the starlit night, lifting a white arrow from the bow. There was a partial moon, just enough light to see the way ahead over the dull shimmering water.

The sea did become calmer as they traveled, and the vessel skimmed over the surface as fast as safety allowed, which seemed way too quick for Terry. He judged, though, that Jeff knew what he was doing. Lights blinked from ships plying the straits and also from mainland Malaysia. Dark shapes of unlit boats also flitted by, and Jeff often had to lurch left or right to dodge one black form or another. Sometimes, for a second or so, the pop-pop-pop sound and fumes of a single-cylinder diesel could be detected as a fishing boat flashed by. Most of them were small wooden boats containing a few men performing their everyday labor of survival. Terry wondered what they could be thinking. What was their view of life? Were they envious of the sleek form briefly cutting through their night? Did they crave a little of the money represented by the streamlined motor cruiser? Or were they indifferent to the modern sights and more interested in the weather and the tides as the daily chore of life ground on?

A number of lighthouses and markers flashed their lonely, regular blinks, though Terry could not tell whether Jeff was using them. Jeff had a more expanded chart clipped to a small chart table nearby, illuminated with a faint green light. After a couple of hours carving through the tunnel of night, Jeff checked the chart and appeared to ascertain the locations of various markers. In those days, GPS systems were both expensive and unreliable, so navigation was done with paper charts and compass bearings.

"It's about time to cross the border," he said. He bought his charge over to port by about sixty degrees in a smooth curve. "Now we're illegal, mate. I hope we don't cop the Indonesian Navy."

"Much of 'em about?" asked Terry.

"Yeah, enough," replied Jeff, not elaborating. "Anyhow, we've gotta talk about what we do when we get to the channel between the island and mainland. We'd better be ready because we want to be outta there again by dawn."

They talked for a good half hour. Then Jeff left Terry with the wheel while he went down to prepare the gear they would need.

With all lights extinguished, they glided through the channel, lying close to Padang Island on their starboard side. The engines hummed mutely underfoot, and the streamlined hull cut through the black water with little sound. There were a few settlements on the island, which they skirted around. There seemed to be enough other traffic for them not to raise too much suspicion. Simple wooden fishing boats, larger steel hulls, and swift speedboats passed by, some with navigation lights on, others off. Nearer the Padang production facilities, Terry felt there would be even more traffic.

Eventually, the production facilities came into view. They were illuminated in a forlorn way. As the field was not the prize it first appeared to be, it was obvious that less attention was being paid to it. Exacom was probably going to let production drop until it was no longer commercial, and then they would pull out, handing it to Pratama.

Jeff used his natural instinct and skill to bring the boat to where they had discussed, an old wellhead some way from the shore-based facilities and out of the loom of the lights and gas flares. They moored directly to the wellhead; a feeble light flashed from its top.

"We're lucky with the tide," observed Jeff. "High and just about starting to turn. We'd better get after it." He had assembled their diving gear on the back deck, and the two of them clambered into it.

"Guys, are you sure this is going to be all right?" asked Lestari. She was now awake and anxiously watching them prepare themselves on the back deck.

"Ask Captain Jeff here," replied Terry. He wasn't feeling at all comfortable about entering the black, silty water to search for some lethal guard of Padang's secrets; however, he tried not to show Lestari his unease.

"Well?" inquired Lestari.

"Should be no probs," answered Jeff, though he too was having his own pangs of discomfort. It was one thing to talk about action in a cozy galley, and another to do it. "I've done more dangerous things, anyway."

"But what about this Jin thing?" asked Lestari. "It sounds pretty dangerous."

"I've got a weapon for Jin," he replied and drew up a long carbon-fiber spear with an odd arrangement of hooks and serrated blades at the end; it looked like a miniature coconut tree.

"Another thing we'll need is these magnetic clampers," Jeff advised. He pulled from a kit bag a couple of heavy cylindrical devices about six inches long, flat on one side. "Like this to clamp." He demonstrated, pointing to a mark. "And turn ninety degrees to unclamp." He put a set into Terry's front pack and another set into his own.

"Who needs weights with these?" commented Terry.

"Yep, that's their other use. Now let's get this line sorted out." He gave Terry a small drum containing a thin line and hook. "One end will be clipped to me; you attach the drum here." He pointed to a fastening on Terry's buoyancy-compensating device. "Feed me out as I move along the pipe. One tug means warning, two means come to me, three means I'm returning, okay?"

"Okay," echoed Terry.

"And here are some lamps for night diving. Put 'em over your head like this, though I don't reckon they'll be any good. It's probably like shark-fin soup down there."

"Don't talk of sharks!" pleaded Lestari.

"Okay. At any rate, don't turn 'em on until we're twenty feet or so down the wellhead."

"How're we going to know about our air?" asked Terry.

"I've got this super gadget here," replied Jeff, lifting his dive computer from where it was fastened. It was quite advanced for the time though quite large. He spent some time adjusting it. The device made some beeps as he pressed various buttons. "Yep, it looks set. I'll assume you breathe a little more than me. It makes beeps and chimes according to depth reached, air remaining, and whether decompression is necessary."

"Fancy thing," remarked Terry. "Does it take away tense nerves?"

"Oh yeah, it does everything, man."

"Then let me touch it," joked Terry, reaching to grab it, trying to ameliorate his fear.

"Terry, I don't like this at all!" burst out Lestari. Terry looked at her. She was understandably quite distraught, and he was sympathetic. He knew, though, that if he showed her even a

136

fraction of his fear, it would make matters worse.

"Well, I don't like being hounded across Asia like some criminal either," Terry said gently. "We've got to find something that will stop that."

"But what if something bad happens?" she asked. "That's not going to be good for anybody either."

"We're going to be careful, don't worry," he said, giving her a hug as best as he could with all his gear on.

"Gotta get goin', mate," urged Jeff, holding up Terry's tank for him to get into. Terry kissed Lestari on the forehead and struggled putting the tank on, and then he provided the same service for his friend. Jeff finally fastened the curious staff to some clips along the left side of his tank so that it stuck up about two meters above his head.

"Jeez, look at us!" said Terry, still trying to master his fear. "Like some weird extraterrestrial invaders."

"We'd probably scare the hell out of anything, the sight of us," answered Jeff. "C'mon." He stepped down the ladder from the dive platform into the water so as not to make a splash.

"Pass my fins," he asked. Terry did so, and Jeff quickly slipped them on and dropped off the ladder fully into the water. Terry followed his example.

"Lestari, pass my fins, please," he asked.

She stayed where she was, arms folded over her chest.

"Lestari!" he pleaded. She slowly reached down and passed him one fin and then another. Her face was composed in the most forlorn expression Terry had ever seen. He hesitated, wondering whether they should abandon the whole misguided adventure.

"Okay?" came Jeff's voice, cutting through his concerns.

"Yep," replied Terry, wrenching himself away. He eased off the ladder into the cool sea. The water on his face brought him back to reality, but Lestari's look still irked him, as though she thought she was going to lose him.

Jeff worked his way around the boat forward to the wellhead, where he waited for Terry.

"Why am I doing this stupid thing?" he whispered to Jeff through gritted teeth.

"Why? Are you scared too?"

"Scared shitless!"

"So am I, but darn, it's exhilarating!" His teeth glowed white, and his eyes flashed as he smiled.

"How is she?" Jeff nodded up at the boat.

"Not too bloody happy," whispered Terry.

"Well, let's get it over. Remember how we'll go?"

"Yep."

They adjusted their masks and took in their regulators, and Jeff disappeared from sight into his spent bubbles. Terry followed when the small length of line he'd payed out between them became taut.

Lestari had heard all they said. She sat alone on the back deck, staring out into the night, tears rolling down her cheeks and falling softly upon the deck.

They moved down the wellhead riser reasonably quickly. Visibility wasn't as bad as Terry had expected. He could just make out the loom of Jeff's lamp when he turned it on, though he was only a meter or so behind. When Terry turned his own lamp on, he could see his watch about a foot in front of his face. This comforted him a little. At least he wouldn't perish in perfect blackness, he thought melodramatically. The fact that Jeff, through years of oilfield diving, probably knew everything that they were likely to encounter served to allay his fears. But then he thought of the dead diver he'd seen on the rig. His heart raced at the image of the white face, open eyes, and blue lips.

With a start, he bumped into Jeff, startling him; he'd not noticed the tension on the line go slack. He tensed in panic and, for a moment, was ready to lunge for the surface. Jeff held his arm, however, until Terry's muscles became less tense. He saw through his mask the "okay" signal made by Jeff's thumb and forefinger and returned the same. Jeff held a magnetic clamper in Terry's mask. Terry realized what Jeff was indicating and took out one of his own to set on the riser to use as a handhold. When this was done, Jeff signaled for Terry to stay and moved off to check that the configuration of the subsea completion was as expected. Terry released the drum of the line and fed it out.

After a short time, he felt two sharp tugs on the line. He released his clamper and tentatively followed the line. This time he didn't surprise his friend and gently brushed against him. He could feel the current gathering strength, however, and visibility was worsening. As time went by, and his eyes could make out less and less in front of his mask, his misgivings increased. He had to exert effort to control his welling fear. It was a claustrophobic hell in the water, and the current clutched at his body like an insidious force trying to wrest away his sanity.

Jeff's pressure on his arm again brought Terry back to reality and calmed him down. He put another clamper into Terry's view mask, and Terry responded by clamping the one in his right hand to the pipe the two were straddling. Their plan was to move along the pipe from the well to the central gathering manifold. When Terry was secure, Jeff went on ahead.

Lestari sat for a long time on the aft deck in her doleful reverie, oblivious to the noises around her. She was finally jolted by a thump on the stern and a chatter of harsh voices. There was the sound of someone clambering up the ladder, and her mouth dropped open.

The head and shoulders of a small, dark, and powerfully built man emerged. Once he registered her, his face twisted with wicked glee.

Lestari gasped. Fear lit her face, and she began backing away. Sensing a pending scream, the invader jumped nimbly up on the rear deck, grasped her arm roughly with one strong hand, and slapped the other over her mouth.

"Don't make any noise, or I slit you open," he snarled in blunt Indonesian.

Lestari stared into his evil black eyes and felt the violence inside. She noticed the ugly gun hitched in a strap around his waist, and the nasty long, curved *parang*, or short sword, swinging on his other side. She guessed he was from the stock of ruthless pirates who terrorized the Malacca Straits at that time. She had read that they would take over the helpless boats of innocent refugees or boat people. They would kill, maim, or rape the passengers wantonly, toss the bodies into the sea after stealing all valuables, and then set fire to the victims' boat before departing. She could see through her fear enough to know she was in big trouble and would have to be very careful. She breathed in deeply.

"Okay?" asked the pirate, feeling his effect on her and sensing her acquiescence. "I said, okay?" he said more harshly, squeezing her arm harder.

Lestari nodded. "O…okay," she stammered.

He relaxed his grip but not his animal stare. He grunted audibly, maintained his nasty smile, and thought of what he could do to this woman. Three accomplices had climbed deftly onto the deck in the meantime. All were similarly attired in black shirts and short trousers. They wore crimson sashes around their foreheads and carried menacing *parangs*. They were sinewy, sun-blackened, and sinister-looking, with pockmarked, weather-beaten faces and broken teeth. One had a gun; a small machine gun hung proudly over his shoulder.

"Who else is here?" demanded the leader, obviously more powerful than the others in his strength of will and body size.

Lestari's mind spun wildly in terror.

"I said, who else is here?" he said more fiercely, again squeezing her arm. The pain focused her thoughts a little better.

"I…er…t…two."

"Is that all? You'd better not lie to me, slut!"

"Ye…yes." She nodded.

"Where are they?"

"D…down, diving."

The pirate's smile widened to reveal a terrible array of broken and decayed teeth. He thought for a few seconds and then turned to his crew.

"They're already looking down below. Too bad for them, the bastards. Search the boat! Majid, guard in case they return!" he ordered in their local dialect. Lestari couldn't understand them at all. Although Bahasa Indonesian is the official national language, there are thousands of local dialects among the Indonesian archipelago, and a single person could not know all of them.

Majid, the one who bore the machine gun, went to keep station at the stern. The other two disappeared to search below decks.

The chief pirate forced Lestari backward into the main

central area and then pushed her into a settee.

"Don't move, slut, or I cut off your tits," he threatened. He moved around the area, checking the small galley, various cupboards, and the chart table. The searchers returned and were ordered to check outside, especially the equipment lockers. "See what's worth taking with us—but we don't want to take too much. We've gotta make these bastards disappear like it was an accident." It was just as well Lestari couldn't understand what they were saying.

The other two returned after a few minutes. They dumped the equipment they wanted to keep on the back deck.

"What to do now, chief?" asked one.

"Go out and watch with Majid. We wait for them to surface," the chief ordered. He then looked maliciously at Lestari. "I'm gonna play a bit." He turned on the soft light of the chart table. "Ah, even more beautiful in the light!" He cackled.

The others smiled knowingly at one another and went outside. The muscular chief advanced on Lestari, glowing with anticipated carnal pleasure.

"I'm gonna fuck you in front of your boyfriends." He chuckled nastily. He grabbed one of her breasts roughly. She gasped and drew away. He quickly slapped her with a backhander across the face. "Don't resist me, slut, or it's gonna be very painful."

She was knocked back onto the settee by the blow, and her lip was cut, swelling and starting to bleed.

He grabbed her crotch outside of her jeans. His other hand was ready to administer another blow if she protested. She was now lying back on the U-shaped furnishing with her legs dangling off the edge. He was standing over her so that despite her desire to draw away, she could not. The hand that was raised for the blow came down and yanked her shirt open and then supported

142

the beast's weight on the back of the settee, while his other hand left her crotch and withdrew his sharp, steely *parang*.

She gasped and froze with terror as he waved the blade millimeters over her skin. He gloated over her fear, feeding off it, excited by it. He moved the blade closer to her smooth skin, just skimming it, as she tried desperately to inhale and make herself thinner. He laughed spitefully and moved the knife over her chest and cut open her bra, flicking the cups away from her breasts. She screamed. He slapped his other hand over her face, driving her head deeper into the cushions.

The watchers outside were drawn to the action by the evil in their own hearts. The two who had searched the boat stood at the entrance to the back deck, enjoying the scene and hoping for some crumbs. Even Majid had moved from the stern and was casting long looks through the windows at the action in the half-lit interior.

With his hand still pressing her face down and supporting his weight over her, the brutal pirate moved his *parang* down her belly again and to her jeans.

Length by length, the two divers worked along the submerged pipe. Jeff tentatively felt ahead, moved forward, brought up a clamper, clamped, and then felt forward again, and so on. The pair moved along the pipe in this fashion for a quarter of an hour. The current was stronger, and it was becoming more and more difficult to maintain a stable position over the pipe. Jeff knew that he must not risk being pulled from his increasingly precarious position and moved forward as low and as close to the pipe as he could. He realized that it was almost time to go back; the tidal current was becoming too strong, and his dive computer had already beeped a time warning.

He decided to make one last length of line, resigned to the failure of the whole silly venture. Feeling forward, though, he felt a fingerlike protrusion from the pipe. He stopped immediately and set a clamper so that he could have a better feel. Further examination showed there was some sort of collar around the pipe, with rubbery fingers every thirty centimeters or so, about as long as his forearm.

Jeff was very careful to avoid exerting much pressure on the protrusions, touching them with only the tips of his fingers. From a side pocket, he withdrew a length of nylon string with a clip at one end. He looped the string about the topmost finger a couple of times and fastened it. He signaled to Terry that he was moving backward, and, as carefully as he could, he withdrew about a meter backward, paying out the other line as he went. This was quite difficult in the current and demanded all his strength and diving experience. When he judged that the end of his lance should be above the collar, he steadied himself with one hand on a clamper, pulled the string as roughly as he could a few times, and waited. Nothing happened.

He tried again with a few healthy jerks, but still, nothing happened. Cursing, he tried some more. Then, after summoning as much strength as he could, he tugged the line one last time and pulled it off completely.

Shit! thought Jeff, unsure whether the line had broken or had become unfastened. He was very hesitant to go forward and check.

But then something struck the end of his staff. As he was unprepared for the force, it unbalanced him, and he lost his grip on his clamper. In desperation, he grabbed again at the clamper and found it but pulled it off the pipe. Fearing he would be dragged into dark oblivion, he desperately thrust himself at the pipe. Whatever it was that had swiped the staff had not let go, so he was able to use this purchase as a support and succeeded in re-clamping to the pipe but very loosely. His legs were carried away with the current. As though suspended from a thin cotton thread, he gingerly withdrew another clamper and clamped it to the pipe. Breathing deeply for a while, he rearranged the clampers so that he could work the staff free from whatever held it. As he struggled, his dive computer beeped urgently that they had only five minutes of air left.

Terry's heart, meanwhile, was pumping at an alarming rate, threatening to break out of his chest. He felt Jeff stop advancing and signal a small retreat. There was then a strange series of tugs and slacks on the line, which left him completely bewildered. He could only fear the worst. In addition, Terry could not control his position in the increasing current. It dragged at his body away from the pipe inexorably.

Finally, he let his legs go with the current, and for a frantic moment, a clamper shifted, and he feared being sucked away completely. It held, however, and he was able to free the other and set it so that he faced into the current, minimizing the drag on his body, hanging on to one clamper with each arm. He arranged the line to go between his arms so that he could feel it run over the arm nearest to Jeff and hence detect any change in tension. He was also aware that it was becoming more and more difficult to breathe, raising new panic signals in his mind. It took all his will to remain in that murky blackness and not break for the surface. He knew that time was running out quickly.

Terry jolted as something touched him, then it felt up his arm. Thank goodness, it was Jeff! An arm pushed him into the pipe, and when Terry was flush against the steel, Jeff worked his way over him and to the other side. He then put one of his clampers away in his front pocket and grabbed the one between

Terry and himself. He set the far one, kicking into the current with his fins as he did so. He then released their common clamper and dragged and re-clamped it.

Terry was dumbfounded in a state of fear for a while and did not follow. Jeff jabbed his arm roughly. The idea Jeff was trying to convey finally jumped into Terry's head, and he moved the far clamper back the way they had come. The pattern being set, they proceeded back along the pipe in three-legged style. Terry began to have serious trouble breathing and didn't think he would make it. His consciousness began swimming as he forced himself to concentrate on the solitary effort of dragging himself back along the pipe. They had, however, gone out very timidly and slowly, so just as Terry was fading and the urge to jettison to the surface became too great, the pair reached the wellhead.

Jeff guided Terry's hand to a belt on his own buoyancy-compensating device and pressed Terry's knuckles around it, indicating that he should hang on. He also fed a strap around the wellhead riser and held both ends firmly. Then, as a linesman might have climbed an electric lamp post using a similar belt, he inflated his buoyancy-compensating device and struck for the surface, hoping that Terry would be able to do the same thing and hang on.

Terry, on his last reserves, had dropped his clamper and was grabbing Jeff's belt with both hands. As they rose, he was able to trigger the inflation of his own device and remembered to keep his mouth open, so that the air in his lungs could pass out as the pressure decreased.

Their ascent was too fast. Jeff fought to keep a grip on the strap with both hands, dreading that it would snag and be torn from his grip. Every breath he drew was an effort. His dive computer beeped its final warning as they made the riser; Jeff was only dimly aware of the sound. It was now silent as he struggled to keep control with his final gram of resolve. The strap stuck on an obstruction on the riser and was snatched from Jeff's hands. The thought of them being dragged for miles with the current or being snared beneath *Sea Speed*'s hull sent enough adrenaline through his veins to hang onto consciousness, and he became aware that they had surfaced! He could see light again!

It was the glow from his own headlamp, now quite dim. He spat out his mouthpiece and gasped cool, clean air. Things were moving fast, though. He bumped against the hull of the *Sea Speed* and was dragged along her length; he didn't have much time to act.

Hoping Terry was still hanging on, he grasped for the handholds on the stern diving platform as they were borne by. Terry's hands were, in fact, frozen in a vicelike grip on Jeff's buoyancy-compensating device as a drowning man would cling to a lifesaver in his last panicked attempt to drag both of them down. He gasped one lungful of air as he realized they were back on the surface, but the next was a mouthful of silty sea water, and his grip relaxed. Jeff grabbed one of Terry's arms and brought it to the handhold. He then thumped him on the shoulder. Coughing and spluttering, Terry slowly regained consciousness. Instinctively, Jeff extinguished both of their lamps.

A piercing, terror-stricken scream split the night and shocked him tense. Cold shivers ran up and down Jeff's spine.

A brutal face stared insidiously down at his victim. She lay naked on the settee, her jeans cut away and thin tracks of blood on her front from crotch to breasts where he'd scored her skin with his knife. Her screams at this stage excited him more. Chortling with evil mirth, he hit her again and then ripped down his own pants. The watchers outside were now intent on the proceedings. Majid's machine gun hung loosely at his side.

The shrill screams also penetrated Terry's returning consciousness. He recognized them as being from his own wife, and he instantly became galvanized for action. Jeff had already yanked off his tank and buoyancy-compensating device and clipped them onto the diving platform. He raced up the ladder with magnetic clampers in each hand. Terry, fueled by adrenaline and the blood-curdling screams, knew that he had to stop whatever was torturing his wife. He somehow managed to squirm out of his own gear and, his mind completely lucid, took another clamper and the staff from Jeff's gear and leaped up onto the back deck.

There are a few men, unfortunately, who are excited by the rape and torture of women and are blinded by lust as they dominate and humiliate females. There are many more men, however, who, when faced with such torture, particularly if it is of a loved one, also lose control, but to a cold naked rage that is much more compelling. It was this rage that consumed both Terry and Jeff. It swelled their every muscle and tendon with extra energy. Perhaps it is strange that, although one rage starts from evil and the other from compassion, both result in violence.

Jeff bounded up the deck and slammed a clamper into the side of the first gun-toting watcher's head, and the man crumpled. Jeff drew back another blow and aimed it at the next one's head. The fellow had a split second to dodge the full impact of the blow, however, and it glanced off his head but didn't knock him out. The third had time to whip out his *parang* and was ready to plunge it into Jeff's ribs. Terry bounded down the deck fairly close behind Jeff and swung his own clamper into the face of the blade-wielding fellow as the weapon was about to strike its mark. The two tumbled into the galley, and Terry, on top, slammed his attacker's head into the floor to finish the job. He then rolled over to see the most wicked visage he'd ever seen; its mouth was open cruelly in terrible rage. His pants were down around his knees, however, and he fumbled to grab his gun belt, which he had cast onto the floor earlier. Terry propelled himself forward and kicked the gun away.

In a bellow of rage, the pirate screamed, "Bastard! Now I'm gonna cut you up slowly!" He still had his *parang* in hand and jumped forward.

Terry's last move had left him in a vulnerable position on the floor, on his back. The pirate kicked Terry's head back and pinned his shoulders to the floor with his feet. Terry saw stars as his head slammed against the floor. Then the blade was at his throat, the evil smile and cold black eyes staring into his face. "Die slowly, white motherfucker," snarled the beast. He cut into Terry's throat, and blood began trickling out.

A gunshot rent the night like a huge thunderclap in the confines of the galley. The side of the pirate's head exploded in red, and he fell sideways and forward, covering Terry with blood.

Lestari held the gun rigidly for a few seconds and then let it fall to the floor. Her face was hard and cold, her eyes firm but glassy. The terror of trauma had passed, and her mind had slipped away to watch as if from a distance like an observer instead of a victim. Calmly, Lestari had retrieved the gun during the commotion and shot her attacker dead.

As the gun clunked on the floor, shouts burst from the back deck. Jeff had been struggling with the second intruder. He was not as much of an expert at fighting as he was at diving, however, and after some struggling, the attacker had managed to stab Jeff in the side. The two had fallen to the floor, with Jeff on the bottom.

The intruder raised his blade for a lethal blow when the gun went off. He started, wondering whether it was he who had been shot.

Absolutely desperate, Jeff grabbed the staff lying nearby and thrust the business end into the fellow's chest. Its blades and hooks caused lacerations enough but tangled in the spines was a piece of rubbery, tentacle-like limb. Its tiny needles snared in the victim's skin and caused a shock of agony. The man screamed in pain and leapt to his feet, blood dripping from his other wounds. He clutched his chest, face contorted in pain, trying to control himself.

Jeff wriggled away and grabbed the machine gun from the deck so that when the wounded attacker controlled himself enough to feel new anger and the desire for revenge, he was staring into a solid gunmetal barrel. He dropped to his knees and doubled up in pain.

"Terry," Jeff called. "Are you all right?"

Terry and Lestari were clutching each other tightly.

"Oh shit!" Jeff said to himself. Every move he made was painful. His own blood was oozing to the deck, and he didn't know how much longer he could keep himself together. "Terry!" he called more urgently, praying his friends were alive.

"Yes, I'm here," Terry called back, not knowing when his wife would fold. He didn't have to worry. The trouble in Jeff's voice came through to her, and she pushed past Terry to go outside.

"Jeff, are you hurt?" she asked, kneeling near him, concerned. He looked at her in alarm.

"Jeez, what have the bastards done to you?" he asked.

"Never mind that; where are you hurt?"

"In the side, hurts like hell. Look, we've gotta get these slime offa here and piss off fast. I'm not gonna be good for much longer."

Terry's mind was working with a sense of urgency. "Can you hang on while I pull their boat alongside?"

"I think so. Just hurry." He turned to Lestari. "You'd better get dressed and cleaned up. There's a medical kit in the locker above the chart table. Get it ready."

She went to follow his advice. By moving and keeping active, she felt she could control the shock that was bound to come.

Terry pulled the other vessel up to the stern diving platform and made it fast to *Sea Speed*'s stern. It was a long, low wooden boat typical of those parts; it had a tiny cabin and a small diesel engine. It was not so large and could be paddled, and the paddles left on the floor revealed how the pirates were able to steal up quietly.

Terry ushered the whimpering, wounded attacker, who was still conscious, into his own vessel and ordered him to the stern, where Jeff could watch him more safely. He then lifted the nearest unconscious figure, manhandled him to the stern platform, and lowered him head first into the other boat. He returned and did the same with the next fellow.

He hesitated, however, and had to gulp to control himself before lifting the lifeless chief out. The bloodied head was grotesque enough but, compounded with the thought of the animal's bestial behavior, Terry felt like vomiting and gagged back a convulsion.

Keep moving, he told himself and dragged the body out by its feet, leaving a trail of blood. The guy was solid, swarthy, and quite heavy. Terry knew he was going to struggle to lift the last body into the wooden boat and didn't really want to touch it any more than he had to. *Bugger it*, he thought, and eased the dead chief straight into the sea.

"Can you hang on a bit more?" he asked Jeff. A look at

his friend's ash-white face worried Terry; he was pretty sick. Jeff nodded. He was not fully conscious of the question. Lestari came out with the medical kit.

"Get that gun, and be ready to use it again," Terry told her.

When she returned with it, Terry grabbed a large machete that their attackers had left on the deck and jumped over into the other boat. Two firm strokes were enough to sever both injector lines on the small diesel engine. He clambered back aboard *Sea Speed* just as the wounded pirate was assessing the potential of an attack, and then he cut the line holding the boats together. The wooden vessel was quickly borne away by the swift current. The eyes of the wounded pirate glinted with enmity before disappearing into the night.

Terry turned to see Lestari bent over Jeff, who had slumped back on the deck, clutching his wounded side.

"Morphine, morphine," he croaked. Lestari dragged up the medical kit and found some syringes marked "morphine" in their plastic seals, ready to go. She forgot her distaste for needles in the moment and cut back the wetsuit to his elbow, using the scissors in the medical kit. She stabbed one of the needles into a vein in his arm and administered a large dose.

"Terry, Terry," he gasped urgently. "We gotta get outta here!"

Terry jumped up and raced up to the flybridge to start the engines. They fired and burbled with assurance. He grabbed the machete again and then ran to the bow. The mooring line was taut because of the current, and a few blows with the heavy blade cut it more swiftly than Terry could release it otherwise. *Sea Speed* drifted broadside to the current as Terry made his way again to the flybridge. When he touched the throttle, the hull surged forward as though also eager to be off. Terry turned toward the direction they had come and gave more throttle. A searchlight cut through the night, reaching toward them. It came from their port side, between *Sea Speed* and the island. Orders barked through a megaphone.

"Stop, stop, Indonesian Navy!"

What the hell! thought Terry. *How long have they been there?* But he was committed now and swung the boat away, pushing the throttle even further forward. The navy vessel was about a hundred meters away; Terry could just make out its shape, a small patrol vessel about double the length of *Sea Speed* but not as sleek.

"Stop! Stop! I said stop!" commanded the voice from the megaphone over the engine noise. Terry swerved one way and then the other. The engines throbbed eagerly with life, and curtains of spray rose from the hull at each turn. The naval vessel had been at anchor and was slow to start.

Terry thrust *Sea Speed* past, and the gap between the boats widened. Machine-gun fire erupted. Terry looked back and saw the spits of flame from the gun. He ducked involuntarily as the bullets whined by. Fortunately, the gunner was not in a stable position as the heavy launch weighed its anchor and gathered way. The gap between the two boats increased to a couple hundred meters, and the searchlight gradually lost contact with its quarry.

Terry turned forward and gasped as the unlit form of a mooring buoy lunged toward him. He managed to yank *Sea Speed* to starboard, and it slipped past, a thin layer of paint to spare. His brow furrowed as he concentrated on shaking off their pursuers and avoiding the many other obstacles in the channel.

At Jeff's insistence, Lestari had given him another shot of morphine. His mind was flying high now, and he babbled incoherently.

"Bastards poison their blades, you know," he mumbled in one lucid moment. "They leave them inside a dead rat's carcass

for a week or so. That arsehole will probably get me in the end."
He winced when the boat swerved this way and that. Even through
his morphine haze, pain stabbed in his side as he rolled with the
motion. The curious lance he'd used to full effect rolled near, its
lethal head still snaring the black tentacle from below.

"Behold the Man-O'-War," Jeff mumbled. "Whatever you
do, don't touch it. Embedded in the rubber are thousands of tiny
needle-sharp barbs, all able to inject a small amount of the worst
poison known to man. If they snag your skin, a painful death is
guaranteed. This one's old, been down there a long time, but I bet
it'll still do the job."

"Who would use a thing like that?" asked Lestari despite
her desire to stop Jeff from talking.

"Someone who wants to hide something in murky water,"
answered Jeff. "You rig a couple of these up with a trigger
mechanism, and anybody who comes near is history. They whip
through the water, snaring whatever is in the way. A spring
mechanism, or even batteries, ensures automatic resetting."

"Save your energy, Jeff. Stop talking," urged Lestari.

"Talking keeps my mind focused," he replied. "Man-O'-
War…came across it off the coast of Thailand. Used by drug
runners at a drug drop. A nasty thing used by nasty people." He
paused and then gasped, "Oh shit, this hurts! Lucky my wetsuit is
keeping me all in."

"I still think you should keep quiet and save your energy,"
said Lestari. "I'm going to get something to make you more
comfortable. Wait a minute." She returned with pillows and
cushions. After making his head and shoulders comfortable, she
placed a pillow over the gash in his side and then, using diver's
webbing, bound his arm and body tightly together. She had to use
all her strength to pass the webbing under his body. Even though
she was being as gentle as she could, he yelled in agony a number

of times. At last, he was braced and supported against the motion of the boat.

"That...feels...a lot better," he mumbled. He swam on the brink of consciousness, his lips moving inaudibly for some time before he finally passed out. Lestari swabbed his face and brow to keep his temperature down and prayed. The urge to help and heal kept her mind focused and shut the door on the swirl of terrifying memories from a few moments earlier.

The naval vessel became less of a threat as Terry wound his way out of the channel, around Padang Island, and into the Straits. He had to concentrate intently, however, to avoid all the flotsam and other traffic. It was as though they were rushing through a tunnel intersected by invisible hazards that could appear at the last second. The game was to not hit anything. Terry had been reasonably proficient at arcade games, and he drew on all his skill and reflexes to prevent smashing into the many obstacles. This time the game was real, with lethal consequences if he got it wrong. The wound on his neck began to throb painfully. *Sea Speed* skimmed on, relishing the free rein.

The sky began lightening from the east after an hour or so. Terry feared dawn would come too soon while they were too far inside Indonesian waters and they would be cut off. As the light grew stronger, however, he could see farther and could coax the boat even faster, as the sea was still quite smooth. She shot along like a bullet, a long, thin line behind scouring their path. This brought a new danger of overturning or catapulting off the larger swells and created a higher level of difficulty. Terry's neck began aching in earnest, impairing his concentration.

The gray light slowly become redder in the east as the sun advertised its intention to rise for another day. Terry heard Lestari yell from the stern. He cut back the speed a little and turned back. She was waving frantically and still shouting. He thought it wise to kill the engines to idle, as there wasn't anything close. He set the auto-helm and went aft to see what his wife wanted, hoping it wasn't too bad.

"Terry, you're hurt," she said when he climbed down to the rear deck. Her face was filled with concern. "I didn't know."

In addition to the blood spattering he had received from the pirate chief, his own blood had been running down his neck and over the wetsuit he was still wearing. It was congealing, but he'd been unwittingly rubbing around the cut so that blood was over most of his face and hands. He also looked haggard from his exertions through the night.

"What's the problem?" he asked.

"Jeff is in poor shape. You'll kill him for sure, bouncing about the place like before. Can't you slow down?"

"We've gotta keep moving; we're still in Indonesia."

"We're not going anywhere until I clean up that cut."

"How bad is it?" he asked. "It hurts like hell."

"Jeff says they poison their knives. Come down here; it shouldn't take long."

After a quick glance around the horizon to assess their safety, he sat down next to the medical kit.

"This is going to hurt," she warned, holding an antiseptic swab. He winced and gritted his teeth as she worked. "Take these painkillers," she offered. He gulped down a few. "And get out of that wetsuit."

He willingly obliged, and after quickly changing into some dry clothes, he felt a lot better. A look at Jeff, however, reignited his sense of urgency. He hoped for all he was worth that his friend would pull through. Dreading the unthinkable, he sprang back up to the flybridge to get the boat moving again. He felt like he had a new set of wings and bent to his task a lot fresher. He urged his waterborne chariot forward again, trying to find the

156

best compromise between speed and comfort to help his seriously injured friend.

Gradually the coast of Malaysia became more than a thin line on the horizon and started gaining relief. Then they began closing in on Singapore. Terry had been studying the UHF radio installed on the flybridge and dialed in the emergency channel noted on the faceplate.

"Singapore Radio, Singapore Radio, this is *Sea Speed,*" Terry said remembering radio drills from his offshore safety courses. He waited for some seconds and then repeated more urgently, "Singapore Radio, Singapore Radio, this is *Sea Speed*. I have an emergency."

This time, after a brief pause, a reply came. "*Sea Speed, Sea Speed*, this is Singapore Radio. Report your position and emergency."

"Singapore, Singapore, this is *Sea Speed*. I am approaching Singapore from the west Malaysian coast. I have a severely injured passenger aboard who will require urgent medical attention."

"*Sea Speed, Sea Speed*, this is Singapore. Please state the nature of the—"

The radio went dead. Terry wondered what could have happened. He tried to call them back. After a minute or two of unsuccessful attempts, they finally returned.

"*Sea Speed, Sea Speed*, this is Singapore Radio, do you copy?" The voice was different than before.

"Singapore, Singapore, this is *Sea Speed*, I copy you loud and clear."

"*Sea Speed, Sea Speed*, this is Singapore Radio. Proceed as quickly as you can to naval pier number 13-A; directions will follow. Under no circumstances berth anywhere else. I repeat, under no circumstances berth anywhere else. Do you copy?" Terry's pulse began racing again as his mind tried to grasp what this could mean.

"Singapore, Singapore, this is *Sea Speed*. I copy loud and clear." Whatever would happen, he had no choice but to obey, else he would risk losing Jeff.

"*Sea Speed, Sea Speed*, this is Singapore Radio. Change to channel four for instructions and copy."

Terry obliged and listened uneasily to what he was required to do. He piloted his sleek charge into Singapore, unable to quiet the qualms in his heart.

CHAPTER 13

There was quite a reception waiting for them when Terry guided *Sea Speed* to a small wooden pier in a quiet corner of the naval dockyard. Two military jeeps and an ambulance stood by; the red light of the ambulance flashed slowly. A couple of marines efficiently fastened *Sea Speed* to the pier, and a few more stood guard with their automatics ready to use. Two ambulance attendants were also on hand, conspicuous in their white uniforms. When the marines had secured the boat, and as Terry was killing the engines, a smart fellow with a peaked cap swung himself on board. He was wearing dark-blue khaki trousers and a lighter-blue cotton shirt with three stripes at the shoulders. He surveyed the back deck from behind tinted glasses, hands on hips, feet apart.

"Hello," he said in a friendly voice as Terry came down from the flybridge. "I'm Captain Lim. I'll be taking care of you from here." He noticed the blood on the deck and paused to observe Terry in more detail. "You have been in a war, have you?" he continued, nodding his head at the mess.

"Yes," replied Terry. "But please help us get my friend to a hospital. He's almost dead."

The officer looked longer at Jeff, whose face had turned a ghastly gray color. Lestari was still swabbing his face and forehead; he was only just breathing. She looked up with pleading eyes.

"Yes, right," clipped the captain. He turned to the waiting

men. "Come on, quickly; get this wounded man off first." The ambulance men and spare marines sprang to obey. One of the paramedics gave Jeff a quick examination and administered a shot in his arm. A stretcher was made up, and swiftly they transferred Jeff to it and bound him tightly. He was then whisked up onto the pier and into the ambulance, attended to by the medic.

"You two had better go also," said the captain, who had observed their injuries. "Hurry! Don't worry about this; we'll take care of it. I'll be in to see you at the hospital."

They clambered onto the pier and into the ambulance quickly, not wishing to delay Jeff's departure for an instant. The rear doors slammed shut, and the vehicle leapt forward, siren blaring and light flashing with renewed frenzy. They didn't have to travel far, as the military hospital, which was their destination, was still within the naval complex, though further inland.

They stopped abruptly in the emergency ambulance bay, the doors swung open, and Terry and Lestari stepped out to allow the attendants to bear Jeff away with all haste. They saw his bed disappearing behind the swinging doors of the casualty theater.

"Please come this way," beckoned another attendant. He showed them to a consultation room and proceeded to get a few personal details. Before too long, another man entered the room. He was of Indian descent and rotund, sporting a moustache. The white clinical coat and stethoscope hanging from his neck bespoke his profession.

"Good morning." He beamed with jovial bedside manner. "I'm Dr. Singh. You are husband and wife, right?" The man who had attended to them earlier left discreetly.

"That's correct," answered Terry, still not sure whether the new medical man was friend or foe.

"Well, which of you is to be first?" asked the doctor. "I say, that cut on your neck looks like it's going bad quickly." Red fingers of infection were spreading down Terry's neck to his chest, like the movement of molten lava.

"How much do you know of why we're here and where we've been?" Terry inquired guardedly.

"Well, nothing, really. Captain Lim ordered me to stand by with a colleague of mine for some injured people who would arrive this morning. I didn't know you were civilians until a few minutes ago. My job is to check you out and make you well. Let's get on with it, shall we? Where did you get that cut?"

Terry hesitated, not knowing whether he would help their cause by telling the truth or not. Finally, he decided it wouldn't matter and gave an abbreviated account of the previous night's adventures, skipping over the attempted rape of his wife.

"Fascinating story," commented Dr. Singh. He was cleaning Terry's wound, getting it ready for a few stitches. "You're very, very lucky to be alive, you know."

"I guess so."

"I've seen cases brought in here, the remains of pirate attacks in the Malacca Straits. Our patrol vessels come across them too frequently. Very, very nasty. The people who do these things are complete beasts. They haven't an ounce of humanity left. It's hard to imagine conditions that can create animals like that." He paused to look at Terry's cut in more detail. "I'm going to have to give you some shots to prevent the infection. You know their knives can carry all sorts of diseases."

"Yes, I've heard," said Terry.

"What about Jeff?" inquired Lestari.

"Oh, I'm sure he will be fine, my dear. My colleague is looking after him. He has the best of care."

"But do you know for sure?" asked Terry.

"Well, not for sure. I came straight here without looking at him. But don't you worry; he'll be all right," assured Dr. Singh.

"Now, I'd better give you those shots right away before stitching."

"I think I should have some too," Lestari said meekly. She was trying to control her welling emotions. She lifted up the windcheater she was wearing to reveal the marks of the pirate's sword across her belly, now blossoming and red.

The doctor was surprised. "Bless my soul, have you been mistreated?" he inquired.

Terry also looked surprised. He hadn't noticed Lestari's cuts in the heat of the night's activities. Lestari couldn't hold the flood of tears anymore. She burst into a fit of sobs, her whole body convulsing, and then she began vomiting. Terry rushed to his wife and held her tight, trying to comfort her. Her body wracked with each wave of emotion, as she bent over, retching onto the floor.

"Let her get this over," said the doctor after the worst of the emotional tidal wave had passed. "Then we'll put her up on the bed. I'd better give her a sedative." He also called for an attendant.

Slowly the convulsions subsided, and with Terry's soothing, they were able to coax her onto the bed while the attendant cleaned up the mess, and the doctor prepared the sedative. "Don't worry, my dear," he said reassuringly. "I'm just going to give you a little needle to make you feel better." This done, he attended her cuts and bruises while Terry stood close by, holding her hand. She was still sobbing. "Are your cuts painful?" asked the doctor gently. She nodded.

"Well, can we have your top off so I can treat them?" he continued. She clutched her arms to her chest, not wanting to be exposed again. Gradually, however, with careful persuasion, Terry was able to lift the garment and reveal her torso. He winced at the thought of what she had endured. The doctor cleaned up the cuts as carefully as he could and applied an antibiotic salve.

"Nothing else, my dear?" he asked. She shook her head no.

"Okay, now let's give you those shots to prevent the poison from spreading further." He prepared the needles and gave them while Lestari clutched Terry's hand. The doctor then asked the attendant to bring another bed so that she could be taken to a ward.

While they were waiting, he sat Terry down in a chair and gave him the necessary injections. The attendant returned with a bed and two bearers, who expertly transferred Lestari to it. She protested at being wheeled away from Terry.

"That's fine," said Dr. Singh, indicating that they should wait. "Wait until I finish with the gentleman. He'll probably need a wheelchair."

He proceeded to put a few sutures in Terry's neck to close the wound. By the end of it, Terry was feeling quite groggy and was happy to be eased into the waiting wheelchair. They were then both wheeled through the confusing maze of corridors, swinging doors, and elevators until finally, the last door opened into a room with two beds. The bearers whisked the now-sleeping Lestari onto her new bed and helped Terry up onto his. The room began spinning almost immediately—he felt so tired. The last thing he remembered before surrendering to inevitable sleep was looking across at the motionless body of his wife.

Consciousness slowly began to return. Terry hovered in that nebulous world of sleep and wakefulness, lightly caressed as if by the languid movement of a calm sea, drawn gently one way and then the other. This dreamy feeling was disturbed when his arm was taken firmly by a figure at his bedside. As reality began flowing back, he became aware of a nurse taking his blood pressure. A thermometer found its way into his mouth, further bringing him around. It was withdrawn, and the nurse read it and made a few notes. Terry was then aware of her bustling around to attend to Lestari. He turned toward his wife and was relieved to see her also move in sleepy response to the nurse's actions. His head throbbed with pain, and he was dazed and disorientated.

"Er...hello," he called to the nurse.

"Oh, hello," replied the nurse in a friendly manner. She was an older, matronly Malay. "Back in the world of the living, are we?"

"Er...I guess so. How long have we been sleeping?" asked Terry.

"Oh, about twenty hours or so," she replied. "You've just missed breakfast, but don't worry, I'll get something to eat organized. Captain Lim wants to see you as soon as you're fully awake."

"Oh yes?" asked Terry, uncertainly.

As good as her word, the nurse sent in some breakfast as the pair stretched and fully awakened. Their experience seemed like some bad dream that had occurred a long time ago. Lestari's eyes were still swollen from her crying, however, and the ugly bruises on her face were now large and a reminder that it was no dream. Terry instinctively felt for the cut on his neck, which removed all doubts about dreaming and reality. He smiled weakly at his wife as they both picked at their food, too groggy to talk. Terry's mind couldn't seem to assemble the most simple of thoughts.

Soon after the breakfast trays were taken away, Captain Lim entered, immaculate and dapper, though minus his sunglasses, which were stored neatly in their case in his top pocket.

"Good morning," he said formally. "How are you both feeling?"

"Dopey, actually," replied Terry. "But a lot better than yesterday."

"That's good," said the captain, sitting himself down on a

chair he dragged between their beds, keeping his back straight in fine military style. After a pause while he assembled his thoughts, he continued. "Now, to be quite frank, you all have caused quite a lot of trouble with your gallivanting about." He looked at one and then the other.

Lestari looked away, but Terry held the captain's gaze. "We had our reasons," he said. "And as they involved the loss of other people's lives, I think they were justified."

"I can't answer for that," replied the military man. "But what you did was highly illegal and carries heavy penalties. Furthermore, you two are very lucky to have escaped as lightly as you have," he said, emphasizing the "you two."

"Why? What about Jeff?" asked Terry, alarmed.

"Your friend was not quite so lucky. He's still fighting for his life. He is strong, though, and I would hope that he'll pull through."

Terry and Lestari looked at each other, their faces mirroring the same concern.

"Fortunately, my commander has a good relationship with his Indonesian equivalent, who has agreed to settle for all the trouble incurred. The Indonesians do, however, request that you return to Indonesia as soon as possible. There is a plane leaving at midday for Jakarta. You will be on it."

He paused for a few moments before he continued.

"I also regret to inform Mrs. Miles that her father has become very sick. I guess she will be needed back in Jakarta, in any case. A man will be here to take you to the airport at eleven o'clock. Please be ready. I hope that we have retrieved all your personal effects." He motioned to their gear, which had been brought from the boat and was neatly arranged against the far wall of their room.

"So, all the best. I hope we can meet in the future under

more pleasant circumstances." He stood up, nodded, and was gone.

Terry and Lestari looked at each other again. She wore new anxiety over her father's condition.

"Well, they've got us good and proper." Terry shrugged. "Whoever 'they' are. And we've got nothing. Bugger!"

They showered and made themselves ready without making much conversation. Both were still woozy after the long sleep and became lost in their thoughts and worries. A nurse appeared to deliver the drugs they would need to be sure any infection was stopped. She also asked the pair to sign discharge forms.

True to the captain's word, at precisely eleven o'clock, a smart young corporal knocked on the door and let himself in.

"Good morning," the young man began. "I'm Corporal Jamal, and I'm to escort you to the airport. Is everything settled?"

"Yep, we're ready," answered Terry. The corporal called in an aide to carry their packs and then strode out and down the corridor, expecting all and sundry to follow. He showed them to a military green sedan waiting at the main entrance to the hospital and opened a rear door for them to enter. Their kit was stowed in the trunk. He then lightly slipped into the passenger seat near the driver, and off they went.

They were taken to the military airport rather than Changi, the commercial airport. Terry couldn't help but be impressed by the fighter aircraft and other military equipment scattered around. After passing through a number of security gates, they drove directly onto the apron and over to a small jet bearing the Indonesian flag. Its lower half was gray and upper half white, the colors of the VIP fleet for high-level government delegations. Two well-dressed Indonesians stood at either side of the entrance steps. Terry and Lestari immediately recognized them as two of the earlier watchers, and their qualms grew. On this occasion, the watchers were all smiles and showed them up the stairs. The men carried their packs into the aircraft and stored them in a rear compartment.

Terry and Lestari were shown to two of the rather plush seats in the narrow fuselage. They looked around and took in the luxurious furnishings and empty seats. Their minders sat a few rows behind.

"Doesn't look like a routine scheduled flight to me," Terry whispered to Lestari. She nodded, still taciturn. "Do you think if I asked for port and caviar, they'd bring it?" he joked, trying to cheer her up.

"I doubt it, my love," she replied, trying her best to respond. "I think we're in the bad books."

He looked outside as the door was closed and the engines were started. After a wave from Corporal Jamal, the unseen pilots fired up the engines fully and went through their checks. As Terry gazed through the small window by his side, the jet began to move forward. It taxied to the end of a runway, turned in to it, and immediately leaped forward as if fired from a catapult. Terry and Lestari were pushed well back into the thick padding of their chairs.

The nose rose, and it launched into the air with brutal energy, a slender arrow cutting through the sky. It banked steeply to the right, still climbing quickly, and clouds began rushing past the windows. In a very short time, it gained cruising altitude and was hurtling toward Jakarta, leaving Terry and Lestari little time to think of the reception that was waiting for their arrival. They were still tired and groggy after their traumas. Their wounds throbbed with muted pain, so they remained in a sullen stupor for the duration of the trip, holding hands for comfort.

CHAPTER 14

The landing in Jakarta was just as hurried. The nose dropped to an alarming angle, and the plane plummeted out of the sky. A few steep turns both left and right were necessary to line up for the approach. Terry and Lestari had to grip their armrests tightly to brace against the centrifugal force resulting from the turns. Clouds flickered by, and then the earth approached rapidly.

Impossibly late, the dive was moderated, the engines muffled to a whisper, and the wheels clunked out. The ground leaped up at them, and Terry drew a breath as their fiery chariot thumped upon the tarmac, which then flashed past at a million miles an hour. Savage deceleration occurred, and the couple was forced forward, restrained by their seatbelts.

Before they dared to draw another breath, the jet attained a more familiar speed while there was still runway left and turned in to a taxiway. The plane had landed at Halim Airport but taxied far away from the commercial terminal to the region used by the air force. The sleek plane was guided to its allotted place, and the screaming engines were shut down. The two Indonesian men came forward.

"We're to escort you to the general's house," said one in Indonesian.

"What about my father?" asked Lestari.

"The general will be able to tell you," answered the fellow.

"Which general?" asked Terry.

"General Siregar, of course."

General Siregar! That was a surprise. The two said no more.

A dark Mercedes drew up to the plane, and the couple were shown into it. One of the men sat in the rear seat between them. Their gear was stowed in the trunk.

"Now, we've been requested that you use these," said the man in the back, drawing out two blindfolds. "Please use them. If you cooperate, there will be nothing to fear."

"Well, I guess we've got no choice," said Terry wryly. The man smiled in acknowledgment and gave them a blindfold each. After checking that both blindfolds were placed correctly, their guard gave the order for the driver to go.

They drove for half an hour or so without making many turns, only traveling as fast as Jakarta traffic permitted. They then began turning and stopping more frequently, as though moving through a suburban area. Terry felt that they were in the Menteng area, once a very fashionable residential area for ministers and diplomats in the center of town. He couldn't tell through which streets they were proceeding, though he reckoned a long-term resident like Lestari might know.

After a final turn right, they stopped suddenly, and the man in the front lowered his window. They were obviously outside an entrance. After a brief exchange with a guard outside, a gate whirred open, and the car proceeded through. It stopped soon after. Terry felt the sunlight fade and guessed they had entered a garage. Another whirring sound behind them confirmed this, as a door lowered and clicked shut.

"Please don't remove your blindfolds yet," requested the man by their side.

The car then began moving downward, to Terry's surprise. It seemed a long time before it gently stopped. After some mechanical clicks and clangs outside the car, they were asked to remove the blindfolds.

Terry looked around, observing nothing but a fairly normal two-bay garage with the car access doors behind them closed.

"You may open the door and exit," the man between them indicated to Terry, who tested the door, found it unlocked, and clambered out. Their guard then let himself out, and Lestari followed.

"Come this way."

They were led through a heavy wooden door into the hallway of what looked like a normal house, albeit one with luxurious furnishings. Paintings and carvings adorned the room, and a large crystal chandelier hung from the high ceiling. Nicely carved and upholstered sofas and chairs formed a pleasant sitting area where guests could be made comfortable. A male servant in an immaculate uniform stood outside one of the wood-paneled doors that opened into the hall.

The guide in front nodded at the servant, who acknowledged with a similar response. He opened the inner door and stood aside.

"Please go in here now; the general is waiting," invited the man.

Terry exchanged glances with Lestari and allowed her to go through first. *To paradise or hell?* he wondered.

After they entered, the door was closed silently behind. They found themselves in a large sitting room, and, at the far end of it, standing up from behind a desk, was no less than General Siregar. He was dressed in a *batik* shirt, dark trousers, and shoes, and also wore a black *peci* on his head. He moved forward to greet them with his arms outstretched. Terry guessed that his dress had been chosen intentionally so that the pair would feel more at ease.

"Welcome, welcome, please make yourselves comfortable," he said, beaming, a set of fine white teeth flashing under his splendid moustache. He motioned to an ornate sofa for them to sit down.

"You are, of course, tired and apprehensive as to why you're here," he continued in perfect English, looking intently from one to the other. Both shrugged affirmatively.

"I am sorry for that and for all that has happened. I hope you believe that." He paused and studied them again. "Nevertheless, I think it is well past time for a little chat so that we can arrive at an understanding about our relative positions. But first, would you like some refreshment? Tea or coffee, perhaps?"

"Coffee, please," answered Terry, craving the boost that caffeine would provide. He was feeling a little ragged. "Lestari?"

"Just water, please," she said with a forced smile. The general turned to the manservant, who had entered quietly behind them. "Coffee for two and water for the lady," he commanded, and the man sprang to obey, leaving through another door.

Siregar made himself comfortable in a master chair, which was arranged so that he could see them both over a coffee table between. There was a pause while he studied the pair, his keen eyes remaining longest on Lestari. He noticed the bruises on her face.

"My dear!" he exclaimed. "I'm sorry that you were harmed. Sometimes the thugs I employ are not very civilized and do not follow orders. How are you feeling now?"

"As well as can be," replied Lestari icily. She did not want this bully to think he could win her over with any superficial show of power and feigned manners. The anger over her degradation still smoldered inside her, and already this mustachioed soldier had admitted partial responsibility. She looked at him directly and asked, "What about my father? We were told in Singapore that he was sick."

"In fact, he's fine," answered Siregar, detecting her hackles and dropping his smile. "A little bending of the truth to ensure that you did not have the urge to disappear again. The point is, he could be sick, and how would you feel if you could not return to Indonesia to be with him?" He looked at them directly and allowed this point to sink in.

She glared at him with a renewed fire in her eyes.

"Ah," he said, diplomatically attempting to diffuse the issue. "I've seen that spirit before, and I recognize it well. But let's look at the situation." He paused while the servant entered and placed the drinks before them on the table. Terry's coffee was in an exquisite silver pot beside an elegant porcelain cup. Lestari's water was in a beautiful crystal glass with a matching decanter. Siregar was thankful for the break to gather himself. The servant retired.

"Okay," he began, his fingers and thumbs forming a triangular temple before him. "Let's get straight to the point. As a Westerner—" he nodded at Terry "—you would appreciate that, and in Sumatra, it is our custom also." He paused again. "To put it bluntly, you have been prying into internal affairs that don't concern you, but these are affairs that benefit Indonesia. We must think of the good of the majority, and what you have been doing can be classed as subversion. You know what penalties that carries?"

"But whatever you think is good for the people is causing loss of life," interjected Terry, not wishing to be intimidated.

"Ah, the brashness of youth," mused Siregar. "Oh, to be young again. But seriously, what development project doesn't cause loss of life? How many people are killed each year in the oil patch alone? Yet it is one of the safest industries. You may shudder if I tell you how many Indonesian workers die per year in the construction industry. The fact that people may die has never been an objection to project development in the past."

"But that's different from deliberately killing them with things like the Man-O'-War," answered Lestari. She sat forward in her seat despite her injuries and was now completely alert; Terry likewise. Siregar stumbled a little; he hadn't expected the conversation to go like this and wasn't comfortable being confronted with the dirty side of his work so directly.

"Well," he began, "our part of the project at Padang needed some protection."

"But what you are protecting is the fact that you are stealing oil," put in Terry. Siregar stopped in his tracks. His smile vanished, and his temper ignited.

"Stealing oil?" he stammered.

"Yes," continued Terry. "It's obvious now that you have tampered with Padang's subsea plumbing to divert a good half of the oil to Pratama's Melati field."

"Stealing oil!" burst out Siregar angrily. His face had colored, and his nostrils flared. "Whose damn oil do you think it is? It's Indonesia's oil! And more specifically, it belongs to the province of Riau and should be used to benefit those people!"

"But Indonesia has agreed to share it eighty percent to twenty percent," continued Terry, undaunted.

"Who agreed?" demanded Siregar loudly. "Some soft technocrats in Jakarta who receive healthy compensation from supposedly non-corrupt foreign oil companies. And where does Indonesia's eighty percent go? In a pipeline down to the same technocrats in Jakarta so that they can further enrich themselves. Look at the oil from Duri, one of the giant oil fields in the world. How much benefit has that given the local people? Very little, that's all. And that is my country. When I was a boy, I looked at that pipeline out of Sumatra and thought it was so unfair that nothing came back. Now I am at last in the position to alter this imbalance, and any time a chance comes to correct these affairs, I tell you, I'm going to take it!" He was stoked up and burning now, but with such earnest conviction, the two subconsciously felt it was better not to stop the outpour.

"And you talk about loss of life? The hospitals and medical care I have provided from the very Padang oil you claim we stole have saved more lives than the few that were lost through its protection. You come in from the West and want to judge us by your own standards. Well, don't!" he stormed, glaring at Terry. "If I were to open up what I've done in Padang to the eyes and ears of all Indonesians, they would salute me!

"And you Westerners are so hypocritical! In you come with your high ideals, criticizing corruption, yet if things don't go your way, who is the first to offer money under the table? How do you think we could do the things we did in Padang with the piping and all the other things necessary to make it work? We found Western people who, for a price, let us know exactly what we needed and concealed other things from being known to others. We also needed someone from high up to help us. Someone whose salary never exceeded a fraction of the Padang development costs. Someone who was coming close to retirement and looking for a nest egg. And we got him too!" he exclaimed, still looking at Terry intensely.

"In Exacom? Who?" Terry asked, fascinated.

"Mr. Ted Marsden! VP of a typically uncorrupt American oil company. He has this very week retired to a fine ranch in the foothills of the Rockies, which he couldn't have afforded in a hundred years of working for Exacom."

Terry's jaw dropped. It was his turn to be lost for words.

"Yes, young man, think about that one," finished the general, allowing the ensuing silence to add to the effect. "More coffee or water?" he asked the two after he had regained his composure. They both declined.

"Now, I'm glad we've got that out. You must be wondering what's going to happen to you. I think it's clear that you are standing in the way of something that I'm committed to." He looked at them, one after the other. Terry stared back at the general's fierce eyes and wondered grimly what was in store. Here was a man who had the will, ruthlessness, and power to get his own way. Siregar saw that he had their complete attention and continued. "What happens to you both is completely up to you, but first I want to tell you a story about a very good friend of mine. Shall I proceed?" he queried. Both Terry and Lestari nodded.

"During our fight for independence, I was labeled as a rebel by the Dutch and forced to live in the jungles of Sumatra with a few other fellows likewise banished. We formed a close-knit group and launched raids on Dutch infrastructure in a guerrilla type of war. I became the leader of this group and formed a very close friendship with a fellow we called Sul, named because he originally came from Sulawesi. In contrast to me, he was a loner and very quiet. He was also very capable and mechanically adept; he could fix anything. Sul became my adviser and confidant as we harried the Dutch out of our country so that we could start running it ourselves.

"As you know, World War II started, and we welcomed the Japanese, who evicted the Dutch. The honeymoon was short-lived, however, as it became very apparent that the Japanese had their own designs on our country, and they forced us Indonesians to feed their war machine. When we came down from the jungles, my group was sent to Plaju, to work in the oil refinery. Sul's mechanical knowledge proved useful to the Japanese. Despite our initial goodwill, we found ourselves being forced to work harder and harder for zero share of the benefits. The Japanese soldiers began showing no respect to us, treating us more like slaves than partners. Some of us, of course, resented this and raised our voices, worked less willingly. This frustrated the Japanese, who pushed harder; we reacted stronger, and so on until matters came to an ugly head.

"One of our original group, a Batak called Robinus, began arguing with a Japanese supervisor and asked him directly how this forced work benefitted Indonesia. The Japanese soldier, so frustrated about our reticence to work, flew into a fit of rage and swiped Robinus across the head with his rifle butt. You know the Batak temper? Robinus lifted himself off the floor, a look of murder in his eyes, and leaped for his assailant's throat. The supervisor panicked and instinctively raised his rifle and fired. He shot Robinus through the head, and his body fell back on the floor in a bloody mess. The Japanese soldier, after a brief pause to collect his senses, reacted more angrily and fired three more shots into the dead man's back, screaming in Japanese. It was clear that he meant 'Let this be a lesson. More of the same to the next who steps out of line.' The shots brought in more Japanese soldiers, who yelled for people to get back to work and pointed their rifles this way and that to prevent a mass revolt.

"Fortunately for them, this occurred in the machine shop, and there weren't too many workers around. In a busier area, the workers would have run amok, I am sure. Sul was there, though, and saw the whole thing. During the afternoon, more soldiers were rushed in, and the atmosphere very quickly became that of a forced labor camp. Our old group gathered together again that night, and we vowed once more never to be the slaves of a foreign power. With a dozen or so other young men, we snuck out from under the noses of the Japanese guards and again took to the jungle. Some of the new fellows were from the region, so we were able to find an abandoned logging hut not too far from Palembang to use as a base. In any case, we had the sympathy of the locals, so it was easy to cover our tracks. Under my leadership and with

Sul's advice, we started training and gathering intelligence on the Japanese—what they were doing, their plans, and so on.

"When I thought we were ready, we planned and executed an ambush on a small Japanese patrol. Everything worked well, and we were successful at securing all their arms. Moving forward carefully and refreshed with confidence from our first success, we became more daring and began to give the Japanese a hard time indeed. It wasn't easy keeping such a band of young hotheads together and disciplined enough to make and execute plans. For this, Sul was invaluable; his quiet manner, common sense, and commitment to our cause always earned respect. We all would listen eagerly to his calm, matter-of-fact voice around a fire at night. He provided an excellent contrast to my own brash style and drive.

"Anyway, we finally planned an attack on the refinery itself. The idea was to detonate a few optimally placed bombs and maximize the damage while minimizing the risks to Indonesian workers. Some of our bombs were primitive devices that Sul and a few of the others who were clever with these things put together. Five of us were to enter the refinery after dark while the others created a diversion nearby. The five were from our original group, myself included.

"To cut a long story short, the fuse mechanism on the device I planted was faulty, and as I was creeping away, the thing went off. I was blown against a pipe and knocked unconscious. I remember being slapped into consciousness by an angry Japanese captain. He was livid with rage, as the rest of the attack had apparently been successful. The refinery was in flames and would be out of action for some time. The Japanese were still frantically getting enough control to arrest the damage and put the fires out. The captain and others were venting their rage on me, beating me and demanding information on my group and our activities. My face became a pulpy mess, and my body was kicked and bruised; I was barely conscious. The captain was quite sadistic and started the worst torture I could ever have imagined. I was stripped naked and tied face down over a table. They then produced a barbed wire whip, which they…" He could not finish and looked away. "It was horrible."

He again paused to dispel the horrific memories and regain his focus.

"When the four remaining rebels of our group rendezvoused at the agreed place, they soon decided I'd been caught, injured, or killed. Sul convinced the others that they should go back into the mayhem and find out for sure. It would be easier to pass in the confusion, and if I was captured, he knew there wouldn't be much of me left after very long.

"Taking control, Sul related a plan of action. Leaving their guns and other conspicuous hardware behind, taking only their knives, they stole back into the burning refinery. People were running hither and thither, ushered by Japanese guards barking orders. It was reasonably easy to work their way to where I was to place my charge and then to the nearest, most likely office where I would be held. The commander's jeep outside the small building indicated that something important was occurring inside.

"Obeying signals from Sul, the group gathered under the dark shadow of some bushes nearby and devised a course of action. They were able to enter the building, slit the throats of all the guards, take their weapons, and burst into the room where I was held. They shot the surprised Japanese and carried me out and into the waiting shadows. You may be surprised by this. How could four men, armed only with knives, take on a dozen well-armed Japanese soldiers and kill every one of them? Well, we had something stronger on our side. It was true that we were well trained and adept in *pencak silat*—Indonesian martial arts—but every man had something else: a magic talisman. Sul in particular had a very powerful one, in the form of a belt he wore around his middle. It was created by an ancient and very strong magic man and had been handed down from father to son through generations. Sul didn't really believe in its power until that night. Since then, I've seen bayonets slash him but never leave any mark.

"So, the four managed to get me out and back to our camp. Times were tough for us after that, as the Japanese clamped down hard in their quest for vengeance. We had to move farther into the jungle. Many innocent people were randomly taken and tortured while being interrogated to reveal knowledge of our whereabouts. Fortunately, I was able to survive. I owe my life to Sul, and much more besides." The general paused, drew a breath, and looked at both of them intently.

"I suppose that you may have guessed I am talking about none other than To'ar Pantou, your father," he finished, turning finally to Lestari.

Terry and Lestari sat in silence, their minds spinning with the tale. Siregar sipped the coffee that was before him and then sat back in his chair, arms upon the armrests. The narration had stirred old emotions within him, and he became lost in his own contemplation. The previous jovial mask had melted away, revealing the real man who dwelled within. His eyes stared absently at some far corner of the room, unseeing, while his attention was turned inside himself.

Terry's analytical mind digested the story and compared it with what he knew. He looked at the general and saw him for the first time as a real individual. Siregar began stroking his moustache unconsciously.

"Excuse me, Pak," Terry began, the first time he'd used the Indonesian term of respect for the older gentleman.

"Er, …yes?" responded Siregar, drawn out of his reverie.

"How, then, do you get to be in your position, whereas Pop, or Sul, has only a very modest existence?"

"Ah," responded the general. "After the war ended and we finally won our independence, things were not perfect. Bung Karno, our first president, despite all that he did in achieving our victory, was not the best manager. He was very good at firing up idealism, drawing us together, and sparking action but not much good at humdrum organization. He wanted the limelight and action but couldn't conjure up the same passion for administration. So, alas, things became disorganized, and rather than power being assigned, it was internally fought over. The military was the most powerful influence in the country, and power was split among various generals depending on their strength and how they fell in Sukarno's favor.

"It was quite a dogfight and not always the case that the best man won. Cowardly opportunists, upon seeing that the coast was clear, tended to grab what they could, often kissing Sukarno's boots for it. Weak and greedy officers, who may have even helped the Japanese, came out spreading stories of their heroic acts and became generals overnight. I know of one spineless turncoat who aided the Japanese, and I'm told by reliable sources he even gave assistance for our capture. Our first camp near Palembang was discovered very soon after the refinery sabotage; luckily, we moved out quickly. That traitor is now one of the most powerful and richest men in the country. Such people have sold our country's resources for their own benefit. They disgust me. Anyway, I'm losing the point." He paused.

"Sul was a very proud man and looked at this mess with disdain. The actions of the greedy, cowardly opportunists made him sick. He had fought for what? To see the foreign master be replaced by some unscrupulous local pigs? He turned his back on it. A few of the players tried to garner his support, knowing that his influence was large. They offered him all sorts of riches, but this only sickened him more, and he insulted all of them by throwing it back in their faces. He left the army and tried to establish a timber business in Sumatra.

"Despite having made some high-flying enemies, he prospered, as you may know. Then came the straw that broke the camel's back. His business partner was coerced by a certain general to cheat Sul and run off with their working capital. At one point after the war, Sul called this particular general a coward to his face when the fellow tried to solicit Sul's support. I know the man; he hasn't changed. We should have killed him while he was helping the Japanese and, before that, the Dutch." Siregar said the last bitterly. His eyes dropped blankly to the floor, and his mind again withdrew inward briefly.

"You know the rest of the story," he said to Lestari, eventually returning to his narrative. "Sul was bankrupt, with a young family to support. I, on the other hand, could not stand by and let our country be carved up without getting part of the action. Sul rejected politics, but I could play the game. 'If you can't beat them, join them, and then beat them' is what I say. So I swallowed my pride and joined the rat pack. I was not as good at playing the game as others, however, and coming from Sumatra didn't help, as most of the emerging powermongers were from Java. Nevertheless, I was respected in Sumatra and kept my support base there. They couldn't take that away from me, though I had to work hard to keep my political influence in Jakarta.

"Sul thought that I had sold out, and we became more and more distant. He was bitterly depressed over the situation and not really open to anybody. I had my own hands full and couldn't spend the time I should have with him. When he became bankrupt, he closed himself off from all of us who were still in the military. He was unreasonable in many ways, not able to listen at all. I went to see him, but he refused me. I sent him an offer of financial support, which he bluntly rejected. I sent him a proposal on how I could use him in the development of Riau, which was still under threat of being taken away. He kept that one, but I heard no word and decided to keep things as they were. Every Lebaran, I send him greetings with a note that my offer is still open. I hear nothing, but I still hope that he mellows in his old age." Siregar shrugged his shoulders and sank deeper into his chair.

"So you're Ban?" asked Lestari, stirring from her own thoughts. "Every Lebaran, we receive flowers from a person called Ban for Pop and his family. We've always wondered who it was, and there's always a letter with the flowers that Pop keeps without showing anybody, though I think Mom knows about it more than she lets on."

"Yes, that's me. Ban is what I was called." He was quiet for some time more but then seemed to catch himself and was reminded of the situation at hand. "Life has its bitterness and sadness," he said, smiling sadly. After a pause, he moved forward in his chair and changed his attitude to tackle the present situation. "So, what's to be done?" He looked again at them both, eyebrows raised, and then addressed Lestari.

"My dear, I owe a lot to your father, and I'm not about to harm his children. I am very sorry that you were hurt. Believe me, I meant just to scare you away. Those lawless pirates took things into their own hands. Perhaps it was fortunate that one of the worst was killed. I'll have to reel them in. I sent a navy patrol boat to see they didn't get out of hand."

"That's odd, then," said Terry wryly. "Because while we were escaping, an Indonesian Navy boat fired upon us."

"Oh, really?" said the general, surprised, raising both his eyebrows and moustache. "They reported that they aided your escape."

Terry shrugged. "The fact is that they fired live bullets at us." He looked at his wife, who nodded in agreement.

"Hmm," murmured the general, looking thoughtfully at the coffee table and stroking his moustache again. "I'll have to find out what happened there." He was genuinely surprised at this news, but Terry caught the ruthless glint in his eye as he mused over the implications.

"There is one other thing to consider," Siregar began again, looking up. "That is your friend Jeff Palfrey. He will need very delicate care to have any chance of pulling through. He is completely dependent on me, and I do want to save his life but also keep my project running. Do you understand?"

Terry looked coolly at the general again. What an odd mix of idealism, violence, drive, compassion, and ruthlessness! After exposing some of his soul, he was still able to draw back and issue a thinly veiled threat. What a tiger!

"We've made some inquiries about Mr. Palfrey, and I am confident he can be discreet. He has led quite a colorful life. I'm sure that if you persuade him to keep quiet, he will keep his word. Rest assured that we will look after him right through to the extent of his employment when, and if, he recovers."

Terry looked at Lestari for support. He was confused, caught between so many opposing influences. His Western ethics didn't help him solve this dilemma. Lestari was perhaps as confused about the ethics but not about the next step. Her priority was her family's protection. It was a typical Indonesian reaction: family first, always, no question.

"We will try," she said, knowing that this implied agreement to the deal Siregar was proposing. She was quite prepared to do this in order to get Terry and her family out of danger. She intuitively felt she had some power over Siregar, knowing better than Terry the intricate web of his Indonesian character. Her acquiescence was by no means a surrender. The general obviously respected her father and had a burning desire to be accepted again by his old friend and be given approval for his swashbuckling methods. She felt that she could use this hold on the general to her advantage. She could not verbalize these feelings, but they made her confident that she and Terry would not become the general's slaves.

"Your secrets are safe with us," she said more strongly, looking levelly at Siregar. "Do you agree, Terry?" She looked directly at her husband with that age-old look wives give when they want their husbands to agree.

Terry looked back at his wife and realized that the inner strength and confidence he knew were in her had been spurred to awaken. He was witnessing a transformation. "Yes, of course," he replied, trying to look the part of the cool Western man, though he was still conflicted and unsure what his wife had in mind, but was perceptive of her confidence.

"*Permisi, Pak* (Excuse me, sir)," Lestari said politely to the general. "I'm very tired, and I would love to see my parents. Can we go now?"

"Why, yes," he replied, surprised, proceeding to get up and show them out of his house like a perfect host. He checked himself and looked at her shrewdly. "A real Pantou," he said, smiling, coming forward to her. "Please give my warmest regards to your father." He kissed her on both cheeks in the traditional way. Terry was surprised to see tears welling in the grand man's eyes.

Siregar then took Terry's hands in both of his. "*Assalamu alaikum*," he said, the Islamic blessing. "Consider me an uncle. Don't hesitate to call if you have trouble." He looked directly at

Terry, and they locked eyes.

In such an emotionally charged state, the young couple were shown to a car and, without the blindfolds, were driven across town to the Pantou house.

The handshaking, backslapping, crying, and embracing of Lestari's family when they returned served to allay Terry's confusion but did nothing to solve it. His Western background and moral framework were not comfortable with this situation. It didn't appear, however, to pose any conflict to the Pantou family. They talked and laughed well into the night, happy to be with each other again. Terry found himself looking at Pop with new insight into the man's history. Pop was, as usual, jovial yet calm, happy to have his family around him. Every wrinkle on his face now seemed to be a furrow of wisdom. At one point, Pop must have felt Terry's gaze and turned to look at him directly. He smiled, his eyes twinkled, and Terry had a glimpse of his mysterious depth. Terry finally excused himself for bed and left Lestari, Pop, and Mom deep in soft conversation.

When he awoke the next day to a clear, bright morning, with all its outside noises and pleasant smells, their recent adventures seemed surreal. He arose from bed, kissed his wife as she slumbered, and went out into the crystal morning light.

The maid brought him a steaming cup of *kopi tubruk*, and he settled down on the front porch to skim through the newspaper. To his astonishment, on the second page was a picture of Siregar, smart in his military attire, opening a fertilizer plant in Riau. The article stated that the gas necessary to supply the plant would be piped from Merani, a new Pratama gas field. On the very next page was another article describing the rapid decline of one of Mobil's gas fields. This article outlined how the company would probably hand over the field to Pratama a lot earlier than expected, as its production fell below economic thresholds. Terry knew that this field was very near Merani.

GLOSSARY

Bapak ("ba-puk")	Title, and mark of respect, for an older gentleman or one with a higher position.
Pak ("puk")	Short for Bapak.
Bajaj ("bah-jai")	Three-wheeled motorized taxi.
Becak ("beh-chak")	Three-wheeled pedicab.
Belanda	Term for white people from the days of Dutch rule (like "Hollander").
Bule ("boo-lay")	White person.
Dilarang masuk	Do not enter.
Kampung ("kam-poong")	Village.
Kopi tubruk ("kopee too-brook")	Black, unfiltered coffee.
Kue lapis ("cooey lapis")	Layer cake made by starting with a first layer, cooking briefly, adding a second layer, and so on until the desired thickness is reached.
Lebaran	The period of one month of fasting for Muslims, which culminates in

the Hari Idul Fitri, or holy day, after the last day. This celebrates the time when Muhammad returned to the people after forty days of fasting in the desert near Medina.

Losmen	Cheap lodgings.
Pagi	Morning.
Peci ("peh-chee")	Headwear for Muslim men.
Permisi ("per-mis-see")	Excuse me.
Pribumi	Like bumiputera, an indigenous person of Malay descent.
Sayang	Darling or love.
Selamat	Greetings.
Wildcat	Exploration well. Originated in the United States, where a well was so far away from civilization that you could hear the wildcats call.

ACKNOWLEDGMENTS

I would like to thank and acknowledge the significant help I have received in producing this book: To my wife Pingkan, Rebecca Smith, Shanley McCray (Opportune Publishing), friend and author, Alicia Young (Aliciayoung.net).

ABOUT THE AUTHOR

Nigel was born in England in 1960, a very good year! His family migrated to Australia in 1964 and moved to a farm just to the east of the coastal town of Albany where he spent most of his childhood years. After primary and secondary school in Albany, Nigel moved to Perth to complete a Bachelor of Science with Honours from the University of Western Australia, majoring in Physics. Instead of becoming a Rocket Scientist, Nigel joined, Schlumberger, a multinational oilfield service company and worked in various roles for 15 years in Indonesia, Australia and Norway. He returned to Perth in 1996 and joined Wapet, an oil company focused on developing Western Australia's oil resources. Chevron absorbed Wapet in 2000 and in 2015 he was transferred to Houston where he currently works.

It was in Albany where Nigel developed a love for the sea. He learned to sail from a young age and it still provides relaxation to this day. "Aqua therapy" is anything to do with the water whether it is sailing boats, windsurfing, kite boarding or stand up paddle boarding. He has sailed over only two oceans but also to and from Antarctica. This love of the ocean is the reason for the nautical symbols throughout the book and website.

Nigel has always been interested in writing despite basing a career on the sciences which he finds more difficult! He has also written and presented technical papers for professional associations within the oil industry. He would have liked to devote more time to writing but found that being married with three active children soaked up all available extra time.

Whilst working on the rigs, Nigel enjoyed listening to and telling great stories. He began Malacca Mystery very early in his career during standby periods and it is an adventure tale set in the backdrop of how things really were in those days!

For more information about the author please visit and contact:

www.pinkstafford.com
info@pinkstafford.com

CPSIA information can be obtained
at www.ICGtesting.com
Printed in the USA
FSHW010906290419
57669FS